THE MYSTERY OF THE
VANISHING VICTIM

**Trixie
Belden**

Your TRIXIE BELDEN Library

Trixie
Belden and the
MYSTERY OF THE
VANISHING VICTIM

BY KATHRYN KENNY

Cover by Jack Wacker

GOLDEN PRESS
Western Publishing Company, Inc.
Racine, Wisconsin

CONTENTS

THE MYSTERY OF THE
VANISHING VICTIM

Mr. Burnside's Surprise • 1

OH, JIM, CAN'T YOU DRIVE any faster?" Trixie Belden pleaded, bouncing up and down on the backseat of the car. Her arms were draped over the front seat, and her head was thrust forward, as though she hoped that would somehow make her closer to her destination.

"I can't go any faster without violating the speed limit—*and* my own common sense," Jim Frayne told her. "This station wagon, handy as it is, is a gas guzzler. Once I get over fifty-five miles an hour, I can practically watch the gas gauge drop."

"Gleeps, Jim," Trixie said, "I wish you weren't always so sensible. After all, we can't burn up that much extra gas between here and Mr. Burnside's house. And I can't wait to see what his surprise is. He sounded so mysterious over the telephone."

Honey Wheeler, sitting in the front seat, next to her brother, widened her hazel eyes when she heard the word "mysterious." But the other young people in the car burst into gales of laughter.

The others included Trixie's older brothers, Brian and Mart Belden, Di Lynch, Dan Mangan, and, of course, Jim Frayne. They, along with Trixie and Honey, were the members of a semisecret club called the Bob-Whites of the Glen. The Bob-Whites were devoted to helping others and to having fun together. Their current project was a community-wide rummage sale to raise funds for the Sleepyside hospital.

The Bob-Whites also kept finding themselves involved in mysteries. Usually, all of the Bob-Whites pitched in to help solve the mysteries, but it was almost always Trixie and Honey who discovered them in the first place. Their love of mystery often led them to suspect something was "mysterious," even when the other Bob-Whites were totally oblivious to it.

"Supersleuth Trixie strikes again," Brian Belden said. Brian was seventeen, a senior at Sleepyside Junior-Senior High School, and the most studious of the Bob-Whites. He was often the first to spot the flaws in his younger sister's logic and to keep her from jumping to the wrong conclusion.

"Our quixotic sibling once again descries suspicious comportment," Mart Belden announced. Mart was Trixie's "almost-twin," just eleven months older and possessed of the same sandy hair, blue eyes, and freckles. His use of enormous words (he hoped) made him seem much older and more sophisticated than he really was.

"All right, all right!" Honey Wheeler's usually soft voice had a note of exasperation in it. She was Trixie's best friend and most loyal supporter, and she hated Trixie's being teased almost as much as Trixie herself did. "You've all had your fun; now I think we should find out what made Trixie think Mr. Burnside's call was mysterious. She usually does have a pretty good reason, you know."

Trixie felt herself blushing at her friend's praise, which was almost as disconcerting as the others' teasing. "What's mysterious is that Mr. Burnside told us to come over and pick up a donation for the rummage sale—no, wait!" She held up her hands to stop any comments. "That's *not* what's mysterious, so don't start laughing again! What's mysterious is that he told me *all* the Bob-Whites *had* to be along when we came to pick it up. He told us we had to come get his donation right away, *first thing*, even though the rummage sale is a week from now. And he told us we *had* to come in the Bob-White station wagon."

"Maybe it's something that's so big and heavy that it will take all seven of us to carry it," Di Lynch guessed. With her violet eyes and black hair, Di was the prettiest of the girls. She was also the most fragile. Trixie bit her lower lip to keep from laughing at the idea of Di Lynch helping to load some heavy object into the car.

"That wouldn't explain why he wanted us to come right away," Trixie pointed out.

"Maybe it's a big, heavy piece of really useless junk that he's extremely eager to get rid of," Dan Mangan said.

"Dan!" Trixie exclaimed reproachfully. "You know Mr. Burnside wouldn't donate a piece of junk to the rummage sale! He's always been very generous. Why, when we had the winter carnival to get books for the school library in Mexico, Mr. Burnside donated all that lumber for a prize, and—" Trixie broke off when she saw the twinkle in Dan's dark eyes and realized that he was teasing her. She grinned at him to let him know she'd caught on to the joke. Dan was the quietest of the Bob-Whites, but he had a lively sense of humor. That was something none of them would have guessed when he had first come to Sleepyside, just at the time the Bob-Whites had been planning their winter carnival. Then he had been sullen and hostile, rejecting the Bob-Whites and clinging to his friendship with a group of troublemakers from New York City. Remembering that time, Trixie was still amazed, and grateful, for the change in Dan Mangan.

"It looks to me as though none of you can come up with a good explanation for Mr. Burnside's mysterious requests," Trixie said. "So I say it's a mystery until proven otherwise."

"And I say it will be proven otherwise very shortly," Jim said, switching on the turn signal as he approached Mr. Burnside's driveway.

Trixie felt a small flutter in her stomach, which she identified as excitement mixed with disappointment. She was eager to find out what Mr. Burnside's donation was, but at the same time, she wanted the anticipation to last a little bit longer. It was the same feeling she had just before Christmas, when she wanted more than anything to find out what was in all those brightly wrapped packages under the tree, but knew that much of the excitement would be over when the presents were opened.

"Whatever Mr. Burnside's donation is, I bet it will be perfectly perfect," Honey declared. "And I bet we'll be really glad that we hurried over here to pick it up."

Trixie looked at her friend gratefully. Honey was so tactful that it sometimes seemed as if she must be able to read minds. What she'd just said was the "perfectly perfect" way to make Trixie feel better.

Jim pulled the station wagon to one side of the circular drive in front of Mr. Burnside's house and shut off the engine. For a moment, nobody spoke. Everyone stared at the huge, white colonial house and wondered what the surprise was that was waiting for them inside. Trixie realized that, as usual, her friends had been just as excited as she was, even though they had tried to pretend that she was getting carried away.

The sound of Jim opening the door on his side of the station wagon was so loud in the silence that Trixie jumped. "We won't find out what Mr. Burnside's surprise is by just sitting here and wondering about it," he said.

With a chorus of "You're right!" and "Let's go!" the other young people piled out of the car and hurried up the sidewalk to the house.

Jim rang the doorbell, and it was only seconds before Mr. Burnside himself opened the door. He looked at the eager-faced Bob-Whites and smiled. "You made good time," he said. "Come on in," he added cordially.

The seven young people crowded through the doorway and walked into the living room. They knew that it would not be polite to seem to be searching the room for the donation; nonetheless,

18

they all stole furtive glances, trying to see something that looked out of place.

It took Trixie only a moment to decide that nothing was *ever* out of place in this room. It was furnished in beautiful, well-preserved antiques. Every bit of wood gleamed, every pillow was puffed and positioned just so. Each coffee table held just enough odds and ends to be interesting without looking cluttered. And while it was formal, it still looked comfortable and "lived in."

"This is a lovely room, Mr. Burnside," Di Lynch said.

Mr. Burnside nodded. "Yes, it is. And I can say that without being immodest, because I really had nothing to do with it. Mrs. Burnside is the interior decorator in the family."

There was a moment of awkward silence. The Bob-Whites were too preoccupied with thoughts of the promised donation to make small talk, but they were also too polite to hurry Mr. Burnside into handing it over to them.

Mr. Burnside, on the other hand, seemed to be in no hurry at all to let them know what the donation was. He rocked back on his heels, surveying his living room with pleasure, as if seeing it through new eyes because of Di's compliment. Finally, he said, "Can I get you young people a soda or something?"

The Bob-Whites looked at one another. There was,

indeed, something they wanted Mr. Burnside to get them, but it wasn't a soda.

Brian cleared his throat as he assumed a take-charge attitude. "Actually, Mr. Burnside, we're sort of curious about the donation."

Mr. Burnside's face broke into a wide smile. "I'll bet you are," he said. "And I think you'll be very pleased with it. You won't blame me for milking it for as much excitement as I can."

The man's frank admission broke the tension, and the Bob-Whites grinned back at him.

"All right," he said. "I'll take you to it. Follow me." He walked straight through to the back of the house and out into the backyard.

Actually, Trixie thought, *backyard* was the wrong word for the expanse of beautifully kept lawn that seemed to go on and on for miles. They were walking toward a garage that stood at the back of the property. Trixie frowned and looked back over her shoulder toward the house. Just as she remembered, there was a two-car garage attached to the house. So this must, instead, be some sort of storage shed.

Mr. Burnside halted a few yards from the shed. "There's my donation," he announced, making a sweeping gesture.

Trixie stared in confusion. She didn't see the donation. There was just the shed with an old car parked next to it.

"Oh, no!" Brian shouted. "Mr. Burnside, don't tell me— You're not—"

Mr. Burnside nodded, the big grin on his face once again. "That's right," he said. "My donation to the rummage sale is a genuine, beautifully restored and working Model A Ford."

Brian let out a long, low whistle, and Trixie took another look at the old car. It wasn't just an old car, she realized now. It was an antique. It was also—it *had* to be—the most valuable donation they had yet received for their rummage sale.

Brian, Mart, and Jim were swarming over the car. Dan Mangan, who shared his Uncle Regan's love of horses over all automobiles, was only slightly less enthusiastic.

Even Trixie and Honey, who were far more interested in mysteries than in motors, had to admit that the car was a beauty. It had a high, square, boxy shape, and alongside the doors, wide running boards that curved up to become the front and back fenders. The wheels had open spokes, like those on a bicycle, and the spare tire was mounted just in front of the door on the driver's side.

"Tell us about it, Mr. Burnside," Brian said as he circled the car, peering closely at every detail.

"Well, it's a nineteen-thirty-one Deluxe Phaeton Model A. The first Model A was built in nineteen twenty-seven, just a few months after Lindbergh

21

made the first solo flight across the Atlantic. And the car caused almost as much excitement as Lucky Lindy did. In some towns, they had to call out the police to control the crowds that gathered to look at the first Model A's."

"It must have created quite a sensation, after the old tin Lizzies," Brian said.

"Tin who-sies?" Trixie asked.

"Tin Lizzie is what they called the Model T Ford," Mr. Burnside explained. "The Model T was a pretty primitive-looking beast, compared to this car. In fact, this Model A was nicknamed the 'Baby Lincoln,' because it looked so much like the more expensive car. But this one cost only five hundred eighty dollars when it was new. There were less expensive Model A's, for as little as four hundred thirty dollars, too."

"Good old Henry Ford was really determined to put the whole country on wheels, wasn't he?" Jim observed.

"He certainly was," Mr. Burnside said. "In fact, before the first Model A appeared, Ford Motors had already manufactured fifteen million Model T's, so he was well on his way to fulfilling that dream.

"You can see Ford's idea of designing a car for people with average incomes by looking at the height of the Model A. It has over nine inches of ground clearance, because Ford was thinking of

22

people who would drive it through the backwoods, on rough dirt roads."

"May I open the hood?" Brian asked.

"Go ahead," Mr. Burnside said. "It opens from the side, and the hood is hinged in the middle. It has a standard three-speed transmission and a single-disc clutch. The first Model A's, the ones built back in nineteen twenty-seven and nineteen twenty-eight, had a multiple-disc clutch that was pretty difficult to manipulate."

Trixie suddenly felt as if she'd been transported to a foreign country. "I can't understand a word you're saying," she told Mr. Burnside.

"Well, I can," Brian retorted. "And I think it's fascinating. Please go on, Mr. Burnside."

"There's a lot more to tell you, but I think it would be better to save it for another time. Right now," he said, turning toward Trixie with a twinkle in his eyes, "let me just add that, although the Ford Company claimed that the car could hit sixty miles an hour, fifty-five is the top speed I've managed with it."

"This is a pretty expensive piece of rummage, isn't it, sir?" Jim asked, his eyebrows pulled together in a worried frown.

Mr. Burnside nodded. "This car is worth several thousand dollars," he said.

"Gleeps!" Trixie exclaimed. She stared at the car

again. "Do you really think anyone will pay that much for it? I mean, I'd hate for the hospital to get less than your donation is worth."

"I wouldn't worry about that," Mr. Burnside told her. "The Model A is a favorite of antique-car collectors. Why, I average at least one call a week from someone who wants to buy the car, and I've never even had it up for sale. That's why I wanted you to come and pick it up right away. I figured you could letter a sign to put on the car, telling where and when it will be sold. If you drive it around town for a few days while you're picking up other donations, you're bound to attract a lot of attention."

"And people coming to the rummage sale to see the car will wind up buying other things! Oh, Mr. Burnside, that's a great idea!" Trixie exclaimed. "I'm glad you said we had to come and get the car right away. Oh, that reminds me—why did you say we all had to come, and why did you say we had to bring the station wagon?"

Mr. Burnside chuckled. "I wanted the Model A to be a surprise," he said. "I didn't want to tell you about it over the phone. But I did want you to be able to take it with you. So I wanted to make sure Brian would be along to drive it. I know he's a pretty good mechanic, and these antique cars can be tricky. I asked you all to come to make sure that Brian would be along, and I asked you to bring the station wagon because otherwise you might have come in Brian's jalopy—and for anyone but Brian, that's every bit as tricky to drive as the Model A."

"That solves the mystery, all right," Trixie said.

"Well, I think there's an even bigger mystery to be solved now," Brian said. "How can you bear to part with this beautiful piece of machinery?"

Mr. Burnside looked solemn for a moment. "I have had a few twinges, I admit," he said. "But there are two reasons for donating the car to the sale. The first one is that I was in the hospital for a couple of weeks last year, and I had excellent care. Donating the car is one way I can express my gratitude.

"The second reason is that I would have had to get rid of the car, anyway. It would be foolish to let it sit outside and rust."

"Why don't you put it in that garage?" Di Lynch asked.

Mr. Burnside lost his solemn look. "The Model A *was* in the garage until last week. Then it lost out—" Mr. Burnside crossed to the garage and raised the door—"to this!"

Trixie blinked. The vehicle inside the garage was the strangest-looking thing she'd ever seen. It stood high off the ground, like the Model A, but it had only two seats, and they were out in the open. The steering wheel stuck up from the front of the car on a long shaft. The wheels of this car were thin, with open spokes that looked like those on a wagon wheel.

Under the car she saw a round, silvery metal tank with faucet handles attached to it.

"It's a Stanley Steamer!" Brian shouted. "Wow! I never thought I'd see one in person."

"In person," Mr. Burnside repeated. "A nineteen-oh-nine Stanley Runabout Model E-two. Two cylinders, ten horsepower, and as fascinating a machine as you'll ever see anywhere."

Brian had already raised the hood, and Trixie stepped forward to look into the maze of piping underneath. "That doesn't look like any engine I've ever seen," she said.

"That's because you've never seen a steam-driven car before," Brian told her. "They were phased out years and years ago. But they were supposed to be wonderful to ride in."

"Would you like a ride?" Mr. Burnside asked.

"Oh, I wasn't hinting," Brian said hastily.

"I know you weren't," the man told him. "But I was kind of hoping you'd ask. I lit the pilot light a while ago, just in case."

"You mean this car has a pilot light like a gas stove has?" Honey asked, wide-eyed.

"It does indeed," Mr. Burnside said. "That's the major problem with these cars: They're wonderful to ride in, but they're a dreadful nuisance to get started. You have to either light the pilot and wait awhile or keep the pilot going all the time, which, of course, is a fire risk.

"And even before I lit the pilot light, I had to make sure there was water in this boiler here. Then I pumped up pressure in these tanks, which hold kerosene for the main burner and gasoline for the pilot light.

"Then I came around to the front here and put the flame from an acetylene torch up to the pilot jet. Once it started to smoke, I opened the pilot valve a little, to let some gasoline in.

"Now I open this other valve here to let gasoline into the main burner to heat it up, just for thirty seconds or so. Then I turn off the gas and open this valve to supply kerosene to the burner. See the blue flame? That means she's burning just fine. All we have to do now is wait for the steam pressure to build up a little. Two hundred pounds will be plenty for us today. If we were going out on hills, we'd need more."

Mr. Burnside climbed into the driver's seat. "Brian, you first," he said.

Brian Belden crawled into the passenger seat with an awed look on his face, as though he couldn't believe what was happening to him.

The other Bob-Whites watched as Brian and Mr. Burnside circled the vast yard in the Stanley

Steamer. Mr. Burnside was talking continually, pointing to gauges and levers. Brian listened, his head turned attentively toward his host.

Trixie shook her head. "It doesn't even sound like a car, does it? I mean, it doesn't make any sound at all."

When the Stanley Steamer returned to the garage, the Bob-Whites gaped in surprise as Mr. Burnside climbed down and Brian took his place behind the wheel!

"Who's next?" Mr. Burnside said. When everyone hesitated, he took Trixie, who was closest, by the arm and almost lifted her into the seat.

Trixie swallowed hard, feeling a bit nervous perched on the high, open seat. But as the car started off, she forgot her nervousness. "It's like floating on a cloud!" she exclaimed.

Brian nodded. "There's no clutch and no gear-shift. There's just this throttle lever. The farther you move the lever, the faster you go. Not having to shift is what makes it so smooth."

After a turn around the yard, Trixie reluctantly gave up her place in the passenger's seat to Jim and went back to stand by Mr. Burnside.

"I can see why the Model A seems less exciting to you, now that you own the Stanley Steamer," she said.

"I'm hooked, all right," Mr. Burnside told her.

"You know, my wife has been an antique collector for years. It started with an old rocking chair her mother gave her, and it took off from there. Now she scours flea markets and antique shops all over the country.

"I used to laugh at her. Then, two years ago, I bought this Model A. Now I've traded up to the Stanley Steamer. I'm not kidding myself that I'll stop there. Why, some of the other people in my antique car club have two or three old cars, and they paid incredible amounts of money for them."

"What does the car club do? I mean, do you have regular meetings and all?" Honey asked.

"Oh, sure," Mr. Burnside said. "We meet once a month at someone's house. We trade information on where to find replacement parts and what kind of car just brought what price at an auction. Mostly, though, the meetings are merely an excuse to show off our cars."

"You all must enjoy that," Honey said.

"We certainly do," Mr. Burnside told her. "The thing is, these old cars really aren't useful as everyday transportation. They're too temperamental, for one thing. They're also too valuable to risk having an accident or exposing them to dirt and rust. So most of us have lots of money—and incredible amounts of time and work—tied up in our old cars. Of course we want to show them off, but except for our annual car show and our monthly club meetings, we don't get much chance to."

Honey murmured something sympathetic to Mr. Burnside, but Trixie drowned her out with a shout of "Gleeps! Mr. Burnside, you just gave me the most terrific idea!"

Trixie's Idea · 2

OH, WOE!" MART BELDEN GROANED. "My sibling's sagacious conceptions invariably discommode all who enter into concurrence, Mr. Burnside. Heed my admonition!"

"Nothing worthwhile is achieved without some trouble, Mart," Mr. Burnside replied calmly. "I'd at least like to hear what Trixie's idea is."

Trixie flashed a look of triumph at her almost-twin, then turned her back on him to speak to Mr. Burnside. "I don't see how this idea could possibly cause anyone any trouble. If you think it will, we'll just drop it right now.

"My idea is this: Since your Model A will be the

31

biggest donation to our rummage sale, and since everyone in town will see it over the next five days while we're driving it around town to get other donations, why don't we make antique cars a big part of the sale?"

"How can antique cars be a big part of the sale when we only have one to sell?" Honey asked.

"We have about fifteen dollars in our club treasury," Dan Mangan said teasingly. "Maybe we could buy a few more antique cars with that."

Trixie gritted her teeth. "Why can't I ever get anyone to understand me?" she asked nobody in particular. "I don't mean *selling* antique cars will be a big part of the sale. *Displaying* them could be a big part of it, though. While the sale is on in the school gym, the people in Mr. Burnside's car club display their cars in the parking lot. Having the display at the same time will attract lots more customers to the sale, so we'll make more money for the hospital— and the car collectors will have a chance to show off their cars!"

"Oh, Trixie, that's a perfectly perfect idea!" Honey exclaimed.

Brian and Jim pulled up to the group in the Stanley Steamer just in time to hear Honey's happy exclamation.

"What's such a perfectly perfect idea?" Jim asked.

Trixie repeated her idea for the two older boys and

waited breathlessly while they mulled it over. Their approval, she knew, would be enough to convince the rest of the group that her idea was a sound one.

Finally Jim frowned and shook his head. "There's something about the idea that I don't like," he said.

"Oh, Jim, what is it?" Honey wailed.

"I don't like the fact that I didn't think of it first." Jim's frown turned slowly into a sly grin.

"Mr. Burnside, do you think the members of your club will be interested?" Brian asked. "The sale is only seven days away. That's pretty short notice."

"A few phone calls is all it will take," Mr. Burnside said. "Why, I could have a dozen antique cars assembled right here within half an hour, if I could promise the owners a crowd to appreciate them."

"Yippee!" Trixie shouted. "Then it's settled. We'll make signs for the sides of the Model A, advertising the show *and* the rummage sale. And we'll call the *Sleepyside Sun* and ask them to put an announcement in the paper about it. I bet we'll be able to raise more than twice as much money as we'd been planning on!"

"I'd say the figure may be four times as much, if Mr. Burnside's Model A sells for anywhere near what it's worth," Brian informed her solemnly. "I must admit, though, I'm a little bit nervous about being responsible for such a valuable item for the next seven days."

33

"The car is well insured, and you're a very responsible young man," Mr. Burnside told him. "If I were worried about the car, I wouldn't be giving it to you."

"One rule I think we should make is that we have the car home safely before dark," Jim observed. "And that means we ought to be heading home right now."

Honey, Di, Dan, and Mart, who hadn't had a ride in the Stanley Steamer, looked crestfallen, but Mr. Burnside quickly reassured them that they were welcome to come back anytime. Reluctantly, the Bob-Whites agreed that it was time to go home.

"I bow to the wisdom of making only diurnal sorties in the Model A," Mart said. "However, I must point out that another controversial decision remains to be made."

"Who's going to ride home in the Model A, and who's going to go in the station wagon?" Dan Mangan asked, finishing Mart's thought for him.

"Well, Brian is driving the Model A, so I'm obviously elected to drive the station wagon," Jim said. "That much is settled, anyway. That leaves five passengers and four seats left in the Model A."

"I'll go with you, Jim," Honey volunteered. "I'm sure that I'll get plenty of chances to ride in Mr. Burnside's car over the next few days."

"I think I'd better choose the station wagon, too,"

Dan Mangan said. "I still have plenty of chores to do for Mr. Maypenny tonight, so the surest means of transportation is the one for me."

"You don't think the Model A will break down, do you?" Di Lynch asked, her violet eyes widening at the thought.

"There's a better chance of it than there is with a newer car," Mr. Burnside admitted. "Automotive engineers had a lot of years in which to make improvements between the time they made my old buggy and the time they made your station wagon."

"Well, then, I'd better take the station wagon, too," Di said. "My parents are going out tonight, and I promised I'd look after the twins. They'll be pretty upset if I wind up stranded in Sleepyside!" Di had not one but *two* sets of twin brothers and sisters, and baby-sitting for them was the way she earned her Bob-White dues.

"Now I only have two passengers for the Model A. Does anyone want to switch back?" Brian asked.

"I will," Honey said. "You don't mind, do you, Jim?"

Her adopted brother shook his head. "I think it was very unselfish of you to volunteer in the first place. But there's no sense missing out on the fun if you don't have to."

Honey Wheeler beamed at the praise from her older brother. For most of her life she had been a "poor little rich girl," an only child whose parents were away on business trips so often that she had been convinced that they didn't love her. All that had changed since the Wheelers had moved to Sleepyside. The friendship that had sprung up immediately between Trixie and Honey had been the start of the change. Finding Jim Frayne, an orphan who had grown up in poverty, and convincing the Wheelers that they should adopt him, had made Honey's happiness complete. Next to her parents, Trixie and Jim were the two most important people in Honey's life, and kind words from them were the most valuable things in the world to her.

Jim patted his sister on the shoulder, waved good-bye to Mr. Burnside and the Bob-Whites who were going home in the Model A, and departed with his passengers.

Mr. Burnside, Brian, and Mart walked over to the old car and talked briefly about how to start it and keep it running.

Trixie shifted from one foot to another impatiently. Once again, she had the feeling that she was listening to a foreign language as "carburetor" and "choke" drifted to her through the twilight. The talk of stalling had made her a little bit edgy. She wanted to be home at Crabapple Farm, with the car parked safely in the driveway.

Finally she heard the engine turn over and begin

idling. Brian called to her and Honey, and they climbed into the backseat, which was so high off the ground that Trixie felt as if she were sitting on top of a hill.

Mart took the front passenger's seat. The four Bob-Whites waved good-bye to Mr. Burnside, Brian put the car in gear, and they started down the driveway.

Trixie forgot her nervousness as soon as they were under way. "I feel as though I were riding in a parade," she said with a giggle. "You know, like the celebrities who sit up on the backs of convertibles and wave to the crowd." She turned to the side and waved regally at the empty sidewalk.

Honey, too, began to giggle at Trixie's pantomime. "It seems to me that the celebrities I've seen in parades have been wearing jeweled tiaras and long white gloves. I don't remember a single one in dungarees and a T-shirt."

Trixie dropped her arm and sagged against the backseat in mock despair. "I guess I'm just not the celebrity type," she sighed.

"Oh, I wouldn't say that," Honey told her. "We're pretty famous around Sleepyside already, for solving all those mysteries. When we're through school and open the Belden-Wheeler Detective Agency, we'll probably get to be even more well known."

"That's right," Trixie agreed. "Why, they'll probably ask us to ride in the Sleepyside Junior-Senior

High School homecoming parade as the most famous graduates of the school. That's all the more reason for me to start practicing now." She turned and waved to the invisible crowds on the other side of the car, while Honey doubled over with laughter.

A sudden swerve of the car made Trixie drop her pose and turn her attention to the road ahead. The headlights caught the reflection of a man in baggy clothes, walking in the road just ahead of them. The man stopped as he heard their car and turned to look at them. He stared after them as they passed.

"Fool hitchhikers," Brian muttered. "He scared the daylights out of me. I didn't see him until we were almost on top of him."

Trixie turned and knelt on the backseat to look at the man. "Maybe we should have stopped and given him a ride," she said.

"In other words, the monitions of our parents have failed to inculcate even a modicum of perception in their distaff offspring," Mart said.

"Moms and Dad have warned me about not taking rides from strangers," Trixie admitted.

"But you, naturally, feel that *giving* a ride to a stranger is a whole different thing," Brian said. "Well, it isn't. And when you get your driver's license, you'll get that side of the lecture repeatedly, believe me."

"It just seems that with four of us and only one of

him—" Trixie began defensively.

"The one of him could be accompanied by a gun that would outnumber all of us pretty effectively," Brian said.

"Pooh! That man didn't look as if he had a gun," Trixie protested.

"What does a man with a gun look like?" Brian retorted.

"I—I don't know. Tough. Mean. That man back there just looked sort of sad and . . . and lonely," Trixie declared.

"A sociopathic murderer might be expected to experience a paucity of companionship," Mart said wryly.

"I just hate to think the world is such an awful place that people can't help other people anymore," Trixie said sadly.

"That's a pretty big conclusion to draw from the fact that it's unwise to pick up hitchhikers, Trix," Brian told her. "There are still plenty of ways to help people, as you, of all people, should know. But you're not responsible for helping everyone, not if it puts you in jeopardy."

"I wish we could talk about something else," Honey said, shivering. "This is reminding me of all the horrible stories they used to tell us in boarding school, to make sure we wouldn't even consider taking a ride from a stranger."

"What kind of stories?" Trixie asked, turning to face her best friend.

"Oh, Trixie, they were perfectly awful! One of the schools I went to was way out in the country, and sometimes we'd get so bored that we'd feel we just had to go to town and browse through the stores or have a soda in a real restaurant.

"But the headmistress would tell us stories of girls who had decided to hitchhike into town and had been murdered or had to jump out of the car because somebody pulled a gun on them." Honey shivered again. "It sounded so awful, I was afraid even to try walking into town, let alone thumbing a ride."

"Do you think the stories were true?" Trixie asked.

"I do," Brian said. "Oh, they may not all have happened to girls from that particular school, but those things do happen, Trixie."

"All right," Trixie said. "You're right and I'm wrong. We shouldn't pick up hitchhikers, and it's a good thing we didn't pick up the man back there."

The four Bob-Whites lapsed into silence, each thinking gloomy thoughts about dangerous strangers.

The silence was broken by two loud backfires from the Model A. And when the silence returned, it was total—the car's engine had died!

Skillfully, Brian steered the coasting car to the side of the road.

"Brian, what happened?" Honey asked nervously.

"I don't know," Brian replied tensely. "I guess this is some of the temperamental behavior Mr. Burnside warned us about." He leaned back for a moment and took a deep breath. Then he opened the door, stepped out of the car, and walked around to the hood.

Trixie looked around to get her bearings and felt a sinking feeling in her stomach when she saw where they were. It was the worst part of Sleepyside to get stalled in: an area of warehouses and boarded-up shops. The nearest public telephone, like the nearest service station, was blocks away. And anyone they might encounter here would not be roaming the streets looking for a chance to be helpful to four stranded young people.

Trixie started as she felt Honey's hand, icy cold, clasp her forearm. She put her own hand over Honey's in what she hoped was a comforting gesture. Trixie was the braver of the two girls, although Honey had changed a lot from the timid creature she'd been when she first came to Sleepyside. But right at this minute, after the scary stories they'd just been discussing, Trixie felt far from brave.

"Can I do anything to help, Brian?" Mart asked. His simple words were, to Trixie, a bad sign. When Mart abandoned his complicated vocabulary, it usually meant he was worried.

"Slide into the driver's seat, and try turning the engine over when I tell you to," Brian replied.

Mart obeyed, and although the engine turned over forcefully, it didn't catch.

Mart and Brian tried four times to start the old car. The last time, the low, slow growl of the engine told them they were wearing the battery down.

Mart turned off the engine and climbed out of the car. He went over and stood next to Brian, and the two boys talked in low murmurs that Trixie couldn't decipher.

After a few moments, the two boys climbed back into the car and sat down.

"What's happening now?" Trixie asked.

"There's a chance that we've flooded the engine. We'll wait a few minutes, then try it one more time."

"And if it doesn't start then?" Trixie persisted.

Brian shrugged, trying to seem casual. "Then we'll have to walk to a telephone and call for help," he said.

"Or we could just sit tight and wait," Mart added. "I think the police patrol this district pretty frequently. A squad car will probably be along shortly."

Trixie shivered as she imagined the two equally unattractive alternatives. Walking through these deserted streets, with all their shadows, didn't sound appealing. But neither did sitting in the car and waiting for the police—or for whoever might come before the police did!

Mart had been fumbling in the front seat, and suddenly he gave a triumphant shout. "I found a flashlight!" he exclaimed.

"Good for you!" Brian said. "I should have thought to look for one. Let's have another look under the hood. If you'll hold the light for me, I might be able to see something that I didn't see before."

The two boys once again climbed out of the car and peered under the hood.

Trixie looked up at the sky. The early summer days were long, but now stars were beginning to appear in the rapidly descending darkness. "We could make a wish," she said, trying to sound jovial.

Honey's voice was barely a whisper in the stillness: "I already did."

"Trixie," Brian called, "we need some help."

"What is it?" Trixie asked.

"It helps a lot to have Mart holding this light for me. So I want you to get behind the wheel and turn the key and step on the starter. Maybe I'll be able to see what the trouble is this time," Brian said.

"Me?" Trixie squawked. "I've never driven a car in my life!"

"I'm not asking you to drive the car! I just want you to turn something and step on something! You've done that before, haven't you?" Brian snapped.

Trixie bit her lower lip as tears sprang into her eyes. She knew that Brian's anger wasn't really at her but at the car and at the dark and at his own sense of helplessness. Still, she was nervous enough, without having someone yelling at her.

Reluctantly, she climbed into the front seat of the car. In her anxiety, it seemed like ages before she even found the key, but she refused to ask for help from her equally anxious older brother. Finally her hand touched the cold metal, and her foot found the starter button on the floor. "I'm ready when you are," she called.

"Now!" Brian called.

Trixie turned the key and stepped on the starter. The engine turned over, but even slower than the time before. It sputtered and almost caught; then it died again.

"I think I've spotted the problem," Brian called jubilantly. "Just hold on a second and try it again when I give the word."

Trixie waited, straining forward, every muscle of her body tensed. She felt as if she were lending all of her energy to Brian, to aid him in getting the car started.

Trixie jerked around when she heard a stifled scream from the backseat, then screamed herself as she saw a man in baggy clothes standing, silent, next to the car.

It was the hitchhiker!

Hit and Run! · 3

FOR WHAT SEEMED LIKE A YEAR, Trixie stared up into the hitchhiker's face. There was a growth of stubble on his chin and upper lip. His face was so thin that the cheeks seemed to have collapsed beneath the cheekbones. Above his long, pinched-looking nose, his thick, dark eyebrows were drawn together in a menacing frown.

Suddenly the eyebrows relaxed, and the thin lips drew back in a smile, revealing crooked teeth. "Sorry. I must have scared the daylights out of you, coming up behind you in the dark," he said in a soft, gentle voice.

Trixie let out her pent-up breath, then slowly drew

it in again. She felt the beating of her heart begin to slow down. "It was sort of a jolt," she admitted.

"I wasn't trying to sneak up on you, you understand," the hitchhiker began.

"Oh, no, I'm sure you weren't," Trixie said quickly, happy to be able to agree with this man who, she was sure, was totally disagreeable.

"It's just that all of our attention was on the front of the car," Honey added tactfully. "You could have galloped up behind us on horseback and we probably wouldn't have noticed you."

The man nodded and turned his own attention to the front of the car. "Are you having troubles with this old machine?" he asked.

The screams had drawn the boys from under the hood of the Model A. Brian answered the stranger's question with a nod. "We just picked up this car from a friend. It's sort of on loan for a few days. He mentioned that it was a bit temperamental sometimes, and we've found out he was telling us the truth. We hadn't gone more than a couple of miles when it conked out."

"It seemed as though the car was just about to start when . . . when you. . . ." Trixie didn't know how to complete the sentence without sounding as if she was accusing the stranger.

"I'm not sure about that," Brian said. "I mean, I got the engine to sputter a little bit, but I'm not sure it was really about to catch. We've worn down the battery so much that I'm afraid to just keep fiddling with the carburetor until something works."

The hitchhiker's bushy eyebrows shot up. "The carburetor, you say?" he asked excitedly. "Let's take a look." He walked around to the front of the car and stuck his head under the hood. "Do you have a flashlight?" he asked.

"Right here," Mart said, turning on the beam and focusing it on the carburetor.

"Mm-hmm," said the stranger. "Just as I thought. Do you have a screwdriver?"

"Well. . . . There might be a toolbox in the car somewhere—" Brian began.

"Never mind," the man snapped. "Do you have a dime?"

The four Bob-Whites all dug into their pockets at once. "Here," Trixie said, coming up with a thin, silver-colored disk and handing it to Brian, who passed it to the hitchhiker.

There was a moment of silence. Then the stranger said, "Uh-huh. Try it now."

Brian looked expectantly at Trixie, but she slid over into the passenger's seat. "This is no time for amateurs," she told her brother.

Brian grinned at Trixie's unexpected caution and climbed in behind the wheel. He turned the key and stepped on the starter. The engine turned and caught immediately, settling into a smooth, purring idle. "It's a miracle!" he exclaimed.

The hitchhiker straightened, rubbing his greasy hands absentmindedly on his pants legs. "It's hardly that," he said. "In fact, it's the simplest thing in the world to someone who's seen a Model A carburetor before. Come here. I'll show you how it works."

Brian got back out of the car and watched and listened as the stranger explained what he had just done.

Trixie scrambled into the backseat again. "Are you as relieved as I am, Honey?" she asked.

The other girl nodded. "In fact, I bet I'm more relieved than you are, because I bet I was more scared than you were when the car wouldn't start."

"Well, you made up for that by scaring me with your scream when you saw the hitchhiker standing next to the car," Trixie told her.

"I'm sorry I scared you, but you must admit that he does look sort of . . . well, disreputable," Honey said, lowering her voice to a whisper to avoid being overheard.

Trixie shook her head. "No. I mean, yes, he does look a little raggedy, but I don't think that's why you were afraid of him. I think we scared ourselves with all those horror stories we were telling right after we first saw him." She held up her hand to stop the protest that she knew Honey was about to make. "I

49

haven't forgotten what was said. I agree with you that both hitchhiking and picking up hitchhikers are dangerous. But, Honey, the point of remembering those stories is to make us cautious, not scared of our own shadows."

Honey wrinkled her nose. "That's true, too. I've heard equally terrible stories of people who have attacked—even killed—harmless strangers because they'd talked themselves into being afraid of them."

"What if we'd hit this guy over the head because we were so sure he was going to hurt us? We'd still be sitting here in a conked-out car, that's what!" Trixie bobbed her head for emphasis as she answered her own question.

"I guess we owe that man an apology," Honey said softly.

"I guess we owe you an apology," Brian said loudly, then turned from the hitchhiker to the girls, who had burst into laughter at his words.

"Oh, Brian," Trixie gasped, "you're always teasing Honey and me about being on the same wavelength, but I guess it's really all of us. We were just saying the same thing!"

"That's right," Honey said. "I'm sorry I screamed when I saw you standing by the car."

"Me, too," Trixie added.

"It's perfectly understandable," the stranger said. "It's dark, and this isn't the safest part of town, I guess." He rubbed his hand across the stubble on his chin. "I guess I'm not the best-looking man in these parts, either. It was my own fault, too, for not saying anything as I walked up. I don't always think about other people's feelings. In this case, I was more interested in the car than the people in it."

"You mean you were wishing we'd given you a ride when we passed you back there," Trixie guessed. "We probably should have, but our parents have told us never to pick up hitchhikers."

The man waved his arm in a gesture of dismissal. "That wasn't what I meant at all. Your parents are absolutely right. You shouldn't give rides to strangers. In fact, if you'll take my advice, you won't get involved with anybody anytime in any way, if you can help it." The man's tone had turned suddenly bitter as he spoke.

"You don't take your own advice, then," Trixie blurted. "I mean, you just got involved with us when you saw we needed help."

The man snorted indignantly. "You're not a very good listener, are you, young lady? I just said it wasn't the people in the car I was interested in. It was the car itself."

Trixie felt herself blushing at his rude rebuke.

"Are cars a hobby of yours?" Brian asked courteously, willing to give the stranger a second chance to be more polite.

"Cars are my hobby, my passion, and, from time to time, my livelihood, young man," the man said.

"Then it must seem strange to be hitchhiking instead of driving," Trixie said.

"I wasn't hitchhiking!" the stranger exclaimed, almost shouting. "You apparently feel so guilty about not giving me a ride that you assume I was asking for one. Well, I wasn't!"

"But you turned to look back at us as we approached, and you stared after us as we went by," Brian pointed out logically.

The stranger snorted again. "If you're going to be driving around town in a Model A for the next few days, as you say you are, then you'd better get used to being stared at. There aren't too many cars on the street today that look like it—or sound like it, for that matter. When I heard that car coming up behind me, I thought I must be dreaming."

"You mean you could tell it was a Model A just from the sound of it?" Trixie asked in amazement.

"Model A or Model T. I couldn't be quite sure. Model A was my first guess, though. There's a slight difference between the two," the stranger said.

"Well, I'm just glad someone came along who knew about the car," Brian said. "We were getting pretty worried."

"I really feel that we should do something to pay back your kindness," Honey said.

"I don't need money," the stranger snapped.

It was Honey's turn to blush, but it took more than a snappish stranger to destroy her tact. "Actually, we don't have much money with us, anyway. I mean that we should do something—give you a ride, or—"

"Aha! Didn't you just say your parents had told you not to go around picking up strangers? Well, listen to them. They know best. And listen to me when I say you shouldn't get involved with anybody if you can help it. That's better advice than what I told you about that old carburetor," the stranger said with a nod to Brian.

Even in the dark, Trixie could see Brian tense. Her oldest brother had a calm, logical mind and a slow temper. But he also had a deep sense of independence and a dislike for being told what to do— especially by strangers. "We'll take our parents' advice about giving rides, but I'm afraid we'll have to reject yours. We happen to believe that getting involved with other people is what life is all about," Brian said firmly.

The stranger stared at the boy for a moment. Then, surprisingly, he started to laugh. "You're strong-willed, I see. I admire that. I won't try to change your mind about people. Maybe life will do that for you, as it did for me. If you still want to do something to pay me back—although, as I said, I did what I did because I like cars, not people—you can tell me how close I am to Glenwood Avenue. Then I'll be on my way—on foot."

Brian relaxed and smiled as the stranger withdrew his unwanted advice. He turned and pointed toward Glenwood and told the stranger the best route for getting there.

The stranger nodded, stuck his hands in his pockets, and started down the street, head lowered, as if he had already forgotten about the Bob-Whites and their Model A and was lost in his own thoughts.

Suddenly, from out of nowhere, Trixie saw the lights of a car. They were moving down the street toward her, and they were coming much too fast. As Trixie turned her eyes away from the blinding lights, she saw, to her horror, that the stranger was walking slowly across the street, directly in their path!

"Hey!" Brian shouted. "Look out!"

But it was too late. The large green van behind the lights sped down on the stranger. A sickening thud told Trixie the van had hit him. She watched in disbelief as the van sped away, not even slowing down. Then slowly, unwillingly, she turned her attention back to the street and the crumpled, motionless form that now lay at the edge of it.

Brian was already racing toward the stranger, and Mart was right behind him. Trixie fumbled for the door latch and finally found it, then stumbled out of the car. Honey scrambled out behind her.

"Is he all right?" Trixie shrieked.

Brian, crouched beside the stranger, looked up at his sister, his face shining white in the darkness. "He's still alive. But a jolt like that has to do some damage. How much, I can't tell."

"What are we going to do?" Honey asked in a strangled voice.

"We need an ambulance, and we need to keep him warm," Brian said.

"I'll find a phone," Mart said as he hurriedly slipped out of his Bob-White jacket and handed it to Brian. Without another word, he was gone, running off down the street.

"It could take ages for Mart to find a phone," Trixie said. "Couldn't we put him in the car and—"

"No!" Brian barked as he took off his own jacket and covered the stranger. "You should know that by now, Trixie. The one thing *not* to do with an accident victim is to move him."

Trixie bit her lip. She *did* know it, but the panic of the moment had driven it from her mind. Once again, she was grateful for Brian's calm reaction to a crisis.

"It's so awful just to sit here with him," Honey said, her voice revealing how close she was to tears.

"I know that," Brian said. "I feel pretty helpless, too. That's why I snapped at you, Trixie. I'm sorry."

"I deserved it, Brian," Trixie told him. "I guess

55

this man was right when he said I'm not a very good listener. But maybe, if people keep telling me the same thing over and over often enough, harshly enough, I'll finally get it through my skull."

"Oh, Trixie, you *do* listen!" Honey hastened to defend her friend. "Sometimes it takes a while for you to think things out—and the rest of us don't seem to be very good at that. Mr. Lytell would never have gotten his money back that time if you hadn't listened. This man was wrong."

"He said we shouldn't get involved with him, either," Brian added. "It looks as if we've got ourselves good and involved with him now."

Trixie looked down solemnly at the twisted body of the stranger. "We don't even know his name," she murmured.

The man on the ground moaned softly and turned his head from side to side. A bleeding gash on his forehead showed in the dim light.

"Just lie still," Brian told him gently.

"Can't," the man panted. "Can't . . . stop. Find. Find the—" He stopped speaking as he tried to raise his head. He groaned in pain and let his head sink back down to the pavement. "Miser," he groaned.

"He has to find the miser? Is that what he said?" Trixie asked, looking from Brian to Honey.

Honey raised her shoulders in a worried shrug, and Brian shook his head. "That's what it sounded like to me, but it's hard to tell," he said. "I don't know if 'miser' was the end of the sentence or a whole separate thought."

"Has anybody heard of a miser who lives on Glenwood Avenue?" Trixie demanded. "The only miser I remember was Jim's uncle, who kept a lot of money hidden in his mattress. But he didn't live on Glen*wood*. He lived on Glen *Road*. Anyway, he's dead now."

"I can't think of any misers in Sleepyside," Brian said. "But then, I know I'm not thinking straight right now. For that matter, our friend here probably isn't, either. Don't take what he says too seriously. And don't get carried away with ideas about tracking down a miser."

Trixie nodded her agreement absentmindedly, staring down at the closed eyes of the stranger. She wondered if the eyes would ever open again. Her own eyes widened, and she reached out to clutch Brian's arm as another thought occurred to her. "I know who we have to track down, and it isn't the miser! It's the green van! That driver just committed a hit-and-run offense. This is a case for the police!"

"I've thought about that," Brian said. "I've thought about how stupid I was not to notice the license number of the van."

"Oh, woe, I didn't think about that, either! I didn't see the driver, and I didn't see the license plate. All I know is that it was a big green van. That's going to be a big fat help to the police!" Trixie said.

"I can add a little bit to that," Brian told her. "I know the make and approximate age of the van. That will be of some help, I suppose. Green vans aren't as common as some kinds of vehicles— although they aren't as rare as, say, a Model A."

Trixie turned and looked back across the street at Mr. Burnside's Model A. "I'd forgotten all about it, too. I know it's silly to think that some inanimate object can be unlucky, but somehow I feel as though we've been jinxed ever since we picked up that car."

"Don't even think it!" Honey said with a shudder. "We still have that car in our possession for seven more days, until the sale. If those seven days are anything like the last couple of hours, I don't think I'll be able to stand it!"

The sound of running feet made all three Bob-Whites start. Trixie rose to her feet when she saw that the runner was Mart Belden. "Did you find a phone? Did you call an ambulance? Will they be here soon?"

Gasping, Mart could only nod in answer to his sister's barrage of questions. He took a few more deep breaths before trying to speak. "I called. . . . On the way. . . . Here soon," he panted.

Even in her state of anxiety, Trixie was aware of

the difference between Mart's tortured, breathless fragments of speech and his usual elaborate way of talking. She was aware, too, of the similarity between Mart's unconnected phrases and those the stranger had uttered a few moments ago: "Can't. Can't . . . stop. Find. Find the . . . miser." Trixie whispered the phrases to herself, trying to repeat as closely as possible the way the man had uttered them.

"I can't stop. I have to find the miser," Trixie whispered, trying the sentences out on her ears. Was that what the man had meant? She narrowed her eyes as she said the words to herself once again. Then she shook her head. Her interpretation made sense, but the problem, as Brian had pointed out, was that there was no way of telling whether or not the words themselves made sense. They might have been just the incoherent ramblings of a badly hurt man.

"How is he?" Mart was still breathing heavily, but he was able to speak clearly once again.

"I don't know," Brian told him. "He's still breathing. His pulse is fairly strong, although it's racing. I suppose he's in shock. He may be bleeding internally. I just don't know."

Once again the Bob-Whites started as a sound pierced the stillness. This time, the sound was the one they'd been waiting for: the wail of an ambulance siren. Behind it was a police car.

Mart stood up and waved his arms to signal the ambulance, which swooped to a halt at the curb. The man and woman who jumped out moved fast and efficiently.

While they examined the stranger, the police asked the Bob-Whites for their names and addresses and what details they could give about the accident.

"Our car had broken down. This man came along and helped me get it started. He asked for directions to Glenwood Avenue. I told him, and he started off across the street. He wasn't looking where he was going. A green van came along and ran him down. The van kept going. We stayed here while my brother went and phoned the ambulance. That's all there is to it," Brian concluded.

"We can move him now," an attendant said. "Let's get the stretcher."

"Can't we go to the hospital, so we'll know how he is?" Trixie pleaded.

"I'd suggest you go home, instead," one of the policemen told her. "There probably won't be any report on this man's condition for several hours. Meantime, we'll give this information to Sergeant Molinson. He'll probably want to hear your story again. I'd suggest you sit tight and wait for him."

Trixie gulped and nodded. She watched silently until the ambulance sped away, with lights flashing and siren blaring, toward the hospital.

"I guess we'd better head home," Brian said. "Our parents are probably frantic by this time."

"I imagine they'll be concerned, all right," Mart said, "but at least they know where we are. I called them from the phone booth right after I called for the ambulance."

"Good thinking," Brian said. "At least that will save us from having to repeat the whole story as soon as we get home. I'd just as soon not think about what just happened for a while—until Sergeant Molinson questions us, at least."

Trixie looked at her brother enviously. He would, she knew, be able to put the incident out of his mind long enough to give himself some much-needed relief. She herself would not be so lucky.

"Honey, do you suppose you could spend the night at our house?" Trixie asked suddenly. "The sergeant will probably want us all together when he talks to us."

"It would be easier for him if we were all in the same place," Honey agreed. Then she smiled wryly. "Besides, I don't want to go home and answer a bunch of questions, either. I'd rather be with other people who don't want to talk about what just happened. I'll call home from your house and ask Miss Trask."

The Bob-Whites drove to Crabapple Farm, the Belden home, in silence. Helen Belden met them at the back door with a worried expression, but Brian stopped her questions with a finger-to-lips gesture.

"We're all right, Moms," he said gently. "And the man who was run down is in the hospital. That's all we want to say about it right now, okay?"

Mrs. Belden opened her mouth to speak, then pressed her lips together and nodded. "Okay," she said.

Trixie threw her arms around her mother and felt the comfort of the familiar embrace. "Oh, Moms, you're wonderful. You understand everything." She pulled away as she remembered Honey. "May Honey stay here tonight?"

Mrs. Belden smiled and put her arm around Honey's shoulders. "Of course you may, dear," she said directly to the honey-haired girl. "I'll call Miss Trask right now and explain."

The two girls went up to Trixie's room and sprawled on the twin beds, staring at the ceiling.

In spite of herself, Trixie saw the scene of the accident replayed in her mind's eye: the stranger turning to walk away, the van, coming out of nowhere, bearing down on him— Trixie sat bolt upright. "That's it!" she shouted.

Honey jumped nervously at her friend's exclamation. "What's it?" she asked.

"When I saw that green van heading for the stranger, I sort of put words to what was happening.

In my mind, I mean. Just now, in my mind, I saw the whole thing again, and I put those same words to it. Both times, I thought of that van as 'coming out of nowhere.' "

"It did seem that way," Honey admitted. "But I don't see what you're getting at."

"You don't?" Trixie asked unbelievingly. "Honey, that van *did* come out of nowhere. No, I don't mean out of nowhere. I mean—out of a parking place! Honey, that van wasn't just coming down the street. It was parked, waiting for the stranger to walk into the street. That man was run down on purpose!"

Unidentified Victim • 4

HONEY WHEELER GASPED and put her hand to her mouth. "Oh, Trixie, you can't mean what you're saying," she said through her fingers.

"I can and I do," Trixie replied. "Think about it, Honey. On that dark, deserted street, we should have noticed that van when it was still blocks away. We should have heard the engine and seen the headlights, even before the stranger started across the street. But we didn't. All of a sudden, there it was, the headlights right in our eyes, blinding us."

"Stop!" Honey cried, burying her face in her hands. "I don't want to think about what came after that. It was so awful!"

"All right," Trixie said gently. "But we have to think about what came *before.* It's important. Sergeant Molinson will want to know."

Honey looked up at the ceiling and took a deep breath, straightening her shoulders. "You're right. I'll think about what happened right up until . . . well, you know." She closed her eyes and sat motionless for what seemed like forever to her ever-impatient detective partner.

Trixie waited, holding her breath, for Honey to play the scene through in her mind. She was eager to hear Honey's conclusion, but she was also proud of her friend for mustering the courage to think about the accident.

When Honey finally opened her eyes, her face remained expressionless. There was neither the gleam of triumph that usually meant she'd decided Trixie was right nor the crestfallen look that meant she'd have to disagree with her best friend. "I don't remember hearing the van or seeing the headlights until it was almost to us," she said. "But I'm not sure that proves anything. I mean, we were wrapped up in what was happening with the car. Then, when the stranger started being nasty and Brian got angry— that took all of my attention, too. I'm just not sure I'd have noticed the sound of a van way off in the distance."

"What about when Brian was giving directions to

Glenwood Avenue?" Trixie demanded. "That wasn't so fascinating, was it?"

"No-o-o," Honey said slowly. "I guess I do remember sort of letting go at that point. You know how you do that when you've been really straining to catch everything in a conversation, and then suddenly you lose interest. It's almost like coming back to your own body. I mean, you suddenly notice how you're sitting and whether you're too warm or too cold. I remember that when Brian started giving directions, I suddenly realized that I'd been sitting with my left foot tucked under me, and it had gone to sleep. So I shifted in the seat to put my foot down on the floor."

"It's amazing what we can remember when we really try, isn't it?" Trixie asked. "When you started talking about your foot just now, I remembered that at that same time, I noticed the handle on the car door digging into my ribs. I leaned back a little bit and rubbed my side with my hand."

Honey nodded. "So, in a way, it's funny that we didn't notice that van earlier; but in another way, I can see how we didn't. It's almost like waking up from a dream. First, all your attention is on the dream. Then you wake up, and for a moment all you're conscious of is just being awake. It takes a while to notice where you are and what time it is and whether the sun is shining and the birds are singing. When I stretched my leg, I was still in that second stage. Maybe a moment or two later I would have heard the van, but that would have been—it *was*—too late. I'll have to think some more about it, though—" She covered her mouth as she yawned— "but I'd rather think about it tomorrow morning. I don't think my thinker is worth very much tonight."

Trixie put her own hand in front of her face as she felt the impulse to yawn rise in her throat, too. She let the yawn come, so broad that it made her jaw ache and her eyes water. "If we knew for sure that Sergeant Molinson wasn't coming over tonight, we could just curl up and go to sleep."

"I may curl up and go to sleep, anyway," Honey said groggily.

The girls were so tired that the knock at the door was not even startling. "Come in," Trixie called in a voice completely lacking her usual vibrant energy.

Helen Belden stuck her head into the room. "Sergeant Molinson just called," she said. "By the time he got through listening to the police officer's report and writing up his own report, he decided it was too late to come out to talk to you young people. He'll be here right after breakfast, though, so I'd advise you to get some sleep."

"That's just exactly what we'll do, Moms," Trixie said gratefully. "Good night."

"Good night, Mrs. Belden," Honey said softly.

Trixie got up and rummaged in her dresser drawer for a spare nightgown that she could lend to Honey. She paused with the nightgown in one hand when Honey said urgently, "Trix, do you know what just happened?"

"No, what?" Trixie asked.

"The phone rang, for one thing. And your mother came up those creaky wooden stairs out there. And we didn't hear any of it!" Now the fearful look of having to contradict her friend was plain on Honey's face.

Trixie handed the nightgown to Honey and, without speaking, began to get undressed.

She was in her pajamas and under the covers before she replied. "I know what you're thinking: If we didn't hear the phone ring or the stairs creak just now, we might not have heard the van then, either. But I don't think it's the same, Honey. This is my own house—and you're here so often that it's practically yours, too. The phone rings ten times a day, and someone goes up or down the stairs a hundred times. Those noises are so familiar, I've tuned them out. I hardly ever notice them, unless I'm expecting a call or expecting someone to come to my door—or hoping they won't."

She grinned at Honey. "I remember when I was making Moms a Christmas present last year. Every little noise in the house made me panicky, because I was afraid Moms was coming up the stairs to bring me some clean clothes or ask me if I was catching a cold or something."

Honey smiled back at her friend. "You don't have to remind me of that," she said. "You finally made me come over and stay here in the room with you, so I could listen for strange noises. Remember?"

Trixie smiled sheepishly. "I remember," she said. "The point is, lots of times we don't hear noises unless we have some reason to. If the doorbell had rung, I'm sure we would have heard it, because we were expecting Sergeant Molinson to come over, not to call. And when we were out there on that deserted street, I think we would have heard almost any noise, because our nervousness would have given us reason to hear it."

Honey Wheeler sighed. "I don't know what to think," she said. "What you say makes sense, but it's confusing having to decide that I *didn't* hear something. I have to remember not remembering, and I can't remember if there's nothing to remember or if I just don't remember what there is to remember. You know what I mean, don't you?"

"Just barely," Trixie teased. Then she added soberly, "I do know exactly what you mean, Honey. All I really have to base my feelings on is that phrase I used to myself, 'the van came out of nowhere.' Maybe it's silly, but I can't just ignore it."

Honey Wheeler made no reply. Her slow, steady breathing told Trixie that she was asleep. Resolutely, Trixie put the thought of the green van from her mind. She rolled over on her side and let herself slide into sleep.

It was another knock on the door that woke the girls the next morning. The knock was followed by a shouted "Shake off your somnolence! Descend and partake of the antemeridian repast!"

"Is that anything like 'come and get it'?" Honey asked, sitting up slowly and squinting in the morning light.

"When you're called to breakfast by Mart, it is," Trixie answered. She threw back the covers and got slowly out of bed, stretching and yawning. "I was going to check out your analogy this morning, Honey. I was going to notice what I noticed when I woke up, I mean. But Mart spoiled it."

"There wasn't much chance to wake up gradually this morning," Honey agreed.

The girls dressed and went downstairs, where the smell of bacon and eggs told them that breakfast was indeed ready. Trixie slid into her accustomed place, and Honey sat in the extra chair that had been set next to Trixie's.

"Morning, everybody," Trixie said, reaching across the table for a slice of toast.

"Morning, everybody," Bobby Belden echoed. "Morning, Honey, most of all. I didn't even know you were here, Honey. You weren't here when I went to sleep last night, were you? You could have read me a story if you were here last night when I went to sleep."

Honey Wheeler smiled down at Trixie's six-year-old brother. "Now, Bobby, you know that if I'd been here last night when you went to bed, I would have read you *two* stories," she told him.

"I know," Bobby admitted. "You always read me two stories or three stories or four stories or—"

"That's enough," Peter Belden told his youngest son gently but firmly. Bobby was at an age when he enjoyed the sound of his own voice, and he would have gone through his entire range of numbers if left to himself.

"Well, you can read me a story after breakfast, anyway," Bobby told Honey amiably.

"I'm not sure that I can, Bobby," Honey said. "Sergeant Molinson is coming over to talk to us this morning, so I may not have time. I'd like to read you a story, though. I promise I'll do my best to make the time."

"You always do your best, Honey," Bobby said approvingly. "Trixie doesn't always do her best, and Mart doesn't always do his best, and Brian doesn't always—"

"Bobby, why don't you pass Honey the scrambled eggs?" Helen Belden asked, interrupting another possibly endless list.

"Okay," Bobby said cheerfully.

"I hope Sergeant Molinson gets here right after breakfast," Trixie said, rushing to get a word in before Bobby started up again. "Now that I'm awake and thinking again, I'm already starting to get antsy."

"The sergeant is usually prompt," Mrs. Belden said. "I'm sure he won't keep you waiting if he can help it."

"I hope he can tell us something about the stranger's condition," Honey said.

"You won't have to wait for Sergeant Molinson to find out about that," Brian told her. "We called the hospital before you two were up this morning."

"Oh, Brian, why didn't you tell us? What did they say? Is the man all right? Can we visit him?" Trixie demanded.

Brian wrapped his arms around his head as if protecting himself from an avalanche. "Whoa!" he shouted. "The hospital said he was in serious condition, which is better than critical but not as good as satisfactory. In other words, he's not in immediate danger, but he's still pretty badly hurt. The only visitors he can have right now are members of his immediate family. And the reason I didn't tell you

I'd called was, I suppose, that I knew I would be letting myself in for the very barrage of questions that I got."

Trixie waved away Brian's last comment impatiently. "If the hospital is only allowing him to see his immediate family, then they must have found out who he is," she said.

"As a matter of fact, they haven't," Brian said. "When I said I wanted to check on the condition of the hit-and-run victim who was brought in last night, the woman on the phone asked me if *I* knew who he was."

"Sergeant Molinson told me last night that one reason he wouldn't be coming over until today was that not finding any identification on the man had caused him a lot of extra paperwork," Mrs. Belden said.

"Then I don't understand," Trixie said. "How can the hospital say that only immediate family members are allowed to visit, if they don't even know who the man is?"

"Never underestimate the convolutions of the bureaucracy," Mart Belden said. "Undoubtedly that phrase is part of the administrative patois, a rationale meant to soften the disappointment accompanying the denial."

"Would somebody translate?" Trixie asked, looking as perplexed as she felt.

"Mart means that the hospital has thought up some stock phrases that sound like good reasons for saying what they say. Just telling me I can't visit someone is too abrupt. Saying I can't visit because I'm not immediate family sounds better, and it would make sense in most cases," Brian said.

"This isn't most cases," Trixie pointed out.

"If the hospital had to teach the volunteers a separate response for each case, volunteering to answer the telephone would turn into a full-time job," Mrs. Belden said sensibly.

"Whoopee!" Trixie shouted.

"We have just heard a response of the type commonly denoted the 'non sequitur,' " Mart Belden said sarcastically. "However, there is, I predict, a rationale for it that my sibling deems rational."

"You bet there is," Trixie said. "When Moms mentioned the hospital volunteers, I remembered that I'm a volunteer there, too. In fact, my day to work as a Volunteen happens to be tomorrow."

"I have a feeling that our stranger is going to get a visit from someone outside the immediate family, whether or not he or the hospital likes it," Brian said.

"Oh, I'll ask permission to see him," Trixie assured him. "But even if they say I can't visit, I'm sure I'll be able to get more information, once I'm there, than we can over the phone."

74

"Sergeant Molinson may have some answers for us, as well as some questions," Honey said.

"Oh, woe! We're right back where we started, waiting for Sergeant Molinson," Trixie said.

As if on cue, the front doorbell rang.

"I don't think we're waiting anymore," Brian said as he pushed back his chair.

"Why don't you four go into the den?" Mrs. Belden said. "Your father and I will clear the dishes."

"Can I go to the den, too?" Bobby Belden asked.

"No, Bobby, I don't think that would be a good idea," Honey said. "Why don't you go up to your room and decide which two stories you want me to read to you after the sergeant leaves?"

Bobby frowned for a moment, but he found it hard to be stubborn in the face of Honey's promise. "Okay," he said, his frown turning to a broad smile.

"You know what's going to happen, don't you?" Trixie said as she and Honey walked to the den. "If you give him that much time to pick out two stories, he's going to find at least a dozen that he 'really, really' wants to hear."

"I'll gladly read him a dozen stories, if I have time," Honey said.

Trixie shook her head. "It doesn't seem fair that I, instead of you, wound up with a little brother. You're so much better with Bobby than I am."

"Well, that's at least partly because I don't see him every single day," Honey reminded her.

In the den, Mart and Brian had already taken their places on the couch. Sergeant Molinson was standing in front of the fireplace. For a moment, Trixie wondered if he was going to remain standing while he questioned them, like a detective in a mystery novel. But the sergeant sat down right after Trixie and Honey did.

"My first question," the sergeant began, "is whether anything ever happens in this town that you young people aren't involved in."

Trixie felt herself beginning to blush, and she stared down at her shoes. It was true that, time after time, when Sergeant Molinson was finishing unraveling a case, he found the Bob-Whites ahead of him. "At least this time you can't accuse us of trying to keep anything from you," Trixie pointed out. "We called the police station immediately after the accident."

"I'm very grateful," the sergeant said wryly. "It was nice of you to want to share this case with my humble department. Now, would you mind repeating your story about what happened last night?"

Brian, grinning at the sergeant's gibe, began the story. He sobered as he described the green van. "It plowed right into the stranger and kept right on going," he concluded.

"About the van," Sergeant Molinson said. "Did you get a license number?"

Brian shook his head. "I'm sorry. It all happened too fast."

"I understand," said the sergeant. "What about the driver?"

Brian looked at Mart, Trixie, and Honey, who all shook their heads. "We can't help you there, either," he told the sergeant. "It was fairly dark, and the headlights blinded us."

Sergeant Molinson sighed heavily. "All right. Let's back up to the victim. What can you tell me about him?"

"He obviously knew a lot about cars," Brian said. "In fact, he told us he did. He said they'd been his livelihood, so I guess we can assume he'd been a mechanic or an automotive engineer at some time."

"But he didn't tell you his name," the sergeant stated in a tone of frustration.

"No," Brian said.

"Did he have any sort of accent that would tell us where he came from?"

"No," Brian replied helplessly.

Once again the sergeant sighed.

"He told us where he was going, though," Trixie said. "That is, he asked us for directions to Glenwood Avenue."

"There are a lot of houses on Glenwood Avenue,"

Sergeant Molinson said. "There are also two restaurants, a laundromat, and a drugstore, as I recall. He could just have been going to one of those places to meet someone."

"Well, it's something," Trixie told him.

"Yeah, it's something. It's a lot of work for my men if I decide to have them check out every place on Glenwood. Well, I've made a note of it, anyway. Anything else?"

"After the man was knocked down, and while we were waiting for the ambulance, he said something. He said, 'Can't. Can't . . . stop. Find. Find the . . . miser.' " Trixie repeated the words exactly as the man had said them.

"Find the miser?" Sergeant Molinson repeated.

"We think that's what it was, but we're not sure," Honey said. "There was that pause between 'find the' and 'miser.' He might have meant it all to go together, or he might not have."

Sergeant Molinson nodded and jotted something in his notebook. "Well, that might be something we can use. Is that it?" He looked around at the four young people.

"There's something else," Trixie blurted. She stopped and looked pleadingly at Honey, wanting her friend's encouragement to tell the others her theory. Honey nodded slightly, and Trixie continued.

"Last night, after we got home, I kept thinking

about the accident. There's something that bothers me about that van. The way I put it to myself was that it 'came out of nowhere.' "

"That's how it seemed, all right," Mart said quietly as he, too, remembered the scene.

"Well, as I thought about that, it seemed to me that a van speeding toward us from blocks and blocks away wouldn't give that impression. But a van that was parked, with its headlights off, just a short distance away, would seem as if it just started toward us suddenly."

"You mean you think someone was parked nearby, waiting for the stranger to cross the street so he could run him down? Trixie, that's ridiculous!" Brian said.

"It isn't ridiculous!" Trixie said hotly.

"All right, then. We'll just call it farfetched," Brian replied.

"What's farfetched about it?" Honey demanded. She'd been willing to admit her own doubts to Trixie privately, but she wasn't about to see her friend's theory scoffed at.

"Well, for one thing, a van pulling out of a parking place at a high speed would have made even more noise than a van barreling straight down the street. We would have heard it," Brian said.

"That would be true if he'd been in a tight parking place," Trixie said. "But those streets were deserted.

79

He could have just pulled ahead slowly, with his headlights off, until he was right on top of us."

"All right," Brian said. "I'll concede that point. But the stranger walked toward us from the opposite direction. How would the driver of the van know the stranger was going to cross the street right then?"

"I'm not saying he did know that," Trixie said. "What if the driver of the van was following the stranger? He saw the stranger stop to help us. He wanted to keep an eye on the stranger, but he couldn't do that if he pulled over directly behind us—and, of course, he couldn't just leave the car in the middle of the street. So he circled the block, or a couple of blocks, and pulled over on the opposite side. He saw you pointing toward Glenwood, and he figured the stranger was about to start walking again. That's when he started pulling slowly out of the parking place. Maybe at that point he didn't intend to run him down. Maybe he was just going to keep following him. Then, for some reason, he changed his mind. He gunned the engine and turned on the headlights, thinking the stranger would be blinded by them and confused. Then he ran him down."

"You paint a vivid picture, Trix, but it just doesn't hold up," Brian said. "Why was the stranger being followed? Why did the driver of the van decide to run him down—especially right there, the only spot for blocks where there would be witnesses?"

"I don't know," Trixie said miserably.

"We can alleviate strain to our credulity, albeit intensify that to our psyches, if we assume that the vehicle was on a random but longitudinal course and we were not cognizant of it," Mart said.

"You mean you think I've made up this whole story because I feel guilty about not having seen the van in time to warn the stranger about it?" Trixie asked.

"It would be more comfortable that way, wouldn't it?" Mart asked simply. "I think we all feel a little guilty about what happened. The stranger stopped to help us, and then we stood by and watched him get hit by a car."

Honey started to cry. "Oh, that's exactly how I feel, Mart! But I didn't know it until you said it."

"I guess I do feel that way, too, Mart," Trixie said. "But I don't think I made up that story to make myself feel better."

"Well, I'd say you folks have no reason to feel guilty," Sergeant Molinson said. "It wasn't your fault. It was the driver's—and the victim's, too. Neither was watching where he was going.

"I can't say I buy your story that the hit and run was intentional, Trixie. But here's something important for you to remember: Hit and run is a crime, whether it's premeditated or not. For that reason alone, we'll put plenty of manpower into finding the driver of that van. Once we find him, we'll be able to find out whether there's some connection between the driver and the victim. If there is, we can start to determine whether the driver had a motive for running the victim down."

Trixie smiled weakly at Sergeant Molinson. "Thanks for taking me seriously," she said.

"Speaking of the connection between the driver and the victim," Brian said, "have you been able to find out who the victim is?"

Sergeant Molinson shook his head. "He had no ID whatsoever on him, and he hasn't regained consciousness long enough to tell us who he is. We took a set of fingerprints, though, and we'll see what the FBI can tell us about those."

"You mean you think the man is a criminal?" Trixie asked.

"Not at all," Molinson said. "It isn't just criminals who have prints on file with the FBI. Their victims often do, too. Some government employees are on file. So are people who worked in defense plants during the war. These days, with all the terrorists taking hostages all over the world, some international companies urge their top executives and their families to be fingerprinted, for identification in case of abduction. And there are many more reasons why people get fingerprinted."

"I hope you can find out who the man is. He might have a family. There might be people miles away who are worrying about him right this minute," Honey said.

Remembering the directions the stranger had asked for the night before, Trixie thought, *Those people might be much closer than we think.*

The House on Glenwood Avenue · 5

WE'LL DO OUR BEST," Sergeant Molinson promised, closing his notebook and standing up to leave.

"We know you will," Trixie told him.

The sergeant paused and peered down at the sandy-haired teen-ager. "We'll want you to do your best, too. You've made a good start by notifying the police of the accident immediately and by telling me everything you know this morning. I'd like you to keep up the good work, as they say. No holding back. Is that a deal?"

Trixie nodded dumbly, aware once again of the trouble she had caused the sergeant in the past—and aware, too, of his genuine concern for her safety.

"The extent of the criminality involved here warrants the involvement of the constabulary," Mart proclaimed. "If our sibling sleuth decides to doubt that, we will gainsay her."

"Thank you, I think." Sergeant Molinson looked quizzically at Mart, left the den, and walked out through the front door.

Just as the front door closed, there was a knock at the back door. Trixie opened it, and Jim stepped inside the kitchen.

"The gang's all here, I see," he said, looking around at his fellow Bob-Whites. "I was beginning to feel absolutely abandoned at home. I decided to come over and get filled in on what happened last night—and to remind everyone that we ought to be putting signs on the Model A this very minute."

"Gleeps!" Trixie shouted, clapping her hand to her forehead. "I'd forgotten all about our rummage sale. We'd better get going!"

"First things first," Jim said firmly. "You owe me an explanation about the events of last night."

"And I owe Bobby two stories, which I'm going to go and read to him right now," Honey said. "I hate to keep going over the story of the accident time after time," she added, almost apologetically, as she hurried up the stairs.

Sitting down at the kitchen table, Trixie, Mart, and Brian told Jim the details of the breakdown of the car, the meeting with the stranger, and the hit-and-run accident.

When they finished, Jim's eyes were clouded with worry. "I feel sort of responsible for what happened," he said. "After all, Mr. Burnside told us that the car was temperamental. It was stupid of me to just take off in the station wagon. I ought to have driven along behind the Model A, to make sure you made it home all right."

"There's no way that's your fault, Jim," Brian told him. "I took responsibility for getting the Model A home. If I hadn't been so sure I could handle it, I would have asked for an escort. So it has to be my overconfidence that's to blame."

"I think we'd just better stop blaming ourselves," Trixie said spiritedly. "Sergeant Molinson said so just a few minutes ago. The driver of that van is responsible. We're not."

"This is a different kind of responsibility, Trixie," Jim said. "I'm talking about the fact that the four of you were alone and frightened on a deserted street, and that you witnessed a really horrible accident. If I'd followed you in the station wagon, that might not have happened. Perhaps it wouldn't have prevented the hit and run directly, though—especially if, as you say, the driver hit the victim intentionally."

"Do you mean you believe my theory about the hit and run?" Trixie asked excitedly. After so much doubt from Honey, Brian, Mart, and Sergeant Molinson, she was thrilled at the thought that Jim might not think her story "ridiculous."

"I believe you believe it," Jim said. "I've seen your hunches be right too many times to dismiss this one totally. I think that what the sergeant said is correct, though: At this point, it doesn't really matter whether the hit and run was intentional or not, because it was a criminal act either way. What's important is that the police will probably look for some connection between the driver and the victim—once they find out who the driver and the victim *are*."

Trixie nodded, but the corners of her mouth were drooping. She'd hoped for real backing from Jim. That wasn't what he'd given her, but she knew it would have to do for now. There was no way of proving her hunch to anyone.

"Well, I think it's high time we turn our attention back to the rummage sale," Jim said. "Now that we have the Model A to sell and the other antique cars to draw a crowd, it seems to me we ought to work even harder to make sure the sale is as successful as possible.

"Since I've had some time on my hands, last night and this morning," he continued, "I took the liberty of forging ahead with the project. I called the *Sleepyside Sun* and told them the antique car show had been added to the sale. The reporter I spoke with was really excited—it turns out he's an old-car buff himself. I'm sure we'll get a good write-up in the paper because of him."

"Oh, Jim, that's terrific!" Trixie crowed.

"I also went over to the clubhouse this morning and lettered two signs to put on the side of the Model A. They might not be as artistic as the ones Honey and Di would have made, but at least they're done."

"Oh, Jim, stop! Now *you're* starting to make *me* feel guilty! You've done everything while we were forgetting all about the rummage sale because of the accident!" Trixie wailed.

"Your turn is coming up," Jim said. "Here's what I started thinking: Our original plan was simply to put up posters around town telling people about the rummage sale and asking them to call us with donations. That would have been fine for a small sale. But now that it's gotten big, I think we ought to go from door to door asking for donations. We have six days. I think we could cover most of the houses in Sleepyside."

"Of course we can!" Trixie said. "Why, almost everyone has a corner of a basement or an attic where they put things they don't want anymore. When the pile gets big enough, or when they think of it, they call a charity to pick it up, or they have a rummage sale of their own. But if we get there first, I bet we could collect a *ton* of stuff!"

"An exceedingly ingenious inspiration," Mart told Jim approvingly.

Jim inclined his head toward Mart in a mock bow. "I had time for just one more step," he said. He reached into his shirt pocket and took out a folded map. "This is Sleepyside-on-the-Hudson," he announced in the tone of a lecturer. "Notice that a series of heavy black lines have been added to the original cartography. These lines divide the town into roughly equal residential districts. Each district is numbered. My plan is that we divide into teams and cover the town, district by district."

"You seem to have thought of everything," Brian said admiringly.

"Oh, no, he hasn't!" Trixie shouted. "I just thought of something else. Let's divide into teams, as Jim said, but let's keep the same teams for the next six days. And the team that collects the most wins a prize!"

"What kind of prize?" Jim asked. "We can't keep any of the proceeds from the auction for ourselves."

"Oh, no! I know that," Trixie assured him. "But there must be something we could put up to make everyone work a little harder—and to make collecting more fun."

"Hmm," Mart mused. "What if the reward for the most diligent team were not pecuniary but temporal?" he asked.

Seeing that no one had entirely understood him, Mart hastened to explain. "Let us say that the winning team will earn five hours' *time* from the team that comes in last—time to be spent in whatever travail the winners designate," Mart said.

"I like that idea," Jim said. "That way, the prize is from the Bob-Whites to the Bob-Whites."

"I also can't think of anything that would make me work as hard as the fear of being Mart's slave for five hours," Trixie added, wrinkling her nose.

"Uh-oh. I just thought of a problem. How do we divide seven Bob-Whites into equal teams?" Jim asked.

"Oh, woe!" Trixie moaned. "Math always ruins everything."

"Just your report card," Brian teased. "I have an easy solution to this math problem. For the next five days, there are really eight Bob-Whites—if we count our friendly Model A. It and I will be a team. The attention I collect by driving through my districts in an antique car should more than offset the problems of working alone."

"Honey and I are the second team," Trixie said.

"I believe that my efforts would be most enhanced by the cooperation of the pulchritudinous Ms. Lynch," Mart said.

"That means that Dan and I will be partners," Jim said. "That's fine with me."

"Let's get started!" Trixie said enthusiastically.

"Mart, call Di. Jim, go tell Dan. I'll go fill Honey in on the plan, and we'll all meet back here after lunch."

"Should we assign districts now?" Jim asked.

Trixie's eyes lit up. "Yes, we should pick our districts right now," she said. She leaned over the map, scanning it for a minute. "There," she said, tapping her forefinger on the map. "That's the district Honey and I choose." She turned and hurried upstairs before any of the others could quiz her about her choice. With any luck at all, nobody would notice that her district contained most of Glenwood Avenue.

Honey, Di, and Dan had been just as enthusiastic as their friends when they were told about the contest to see which team raised the most donations. Honey was excited, too, about the chance to do some sleuthing while they made their rounds.

None of the others said anything about the fact that Trixie and Honey's district included Glenwood Avenue—until the girls climbed out of the station wagon to begin canvassing.

"Good luck," Jim said then. "And remember, there're five hours of hard labor at stake here. Don't get so caught up in trying to figure out where the stranger was going last night that you forget our primary reason for being here."

Trixie stamped her feet impatiently. "You knew all along," she said.

"I figured it out even before you pointed at this district on the map. I could tell from the way your eyes lit up that you were on the trail of a mystery. But I know better than to try to keep Belden and Wheeler from 'detective-izing.' So, as I said, good luck. But don't lose sight of our real reason for being out here today."

"We won't," Honey assured him. "We won't forget that the hospital is counting on us to raise lots of money with our rummage sale. And we sure won't forget the consequences if our team loses!"

"I can't ask for anything more," Jim said with a grin, "except that you be waiting here when I come back for you at five o'clock."

The girls nodded their agreement and waved goodbye to Jim and Dan, who were the last two Bob-Whites to head for their district.

"Time's a-wasting," Trixie said as she headed for the nearest house. "Brian left in the Model A at the same time we started out in the station wagon, so he's probably already got the attention of half the people in his district. And since Mart and Di were dropped off before we were, they've probably finished at least one house already."

Honey giggled at Trixie's worried calculations. "We have six whole days to make collections, Trix," she said. "I don't think we're in too much danger of losing the contest in the first six minutes!"

Trixie grinned sheepishly, but she put a resolute finger to the doorbell without saying anything more.

The girls heard the bell reverberating through the house, and a few seconds later they heard footsteps approaching on the other side of the door.

"Yes?" A middle-aged woman with neatly combed gray hair spoke to them through the screen door.

"Hi," Trixie said. "My name is Trixie Belden, and this is my friend Honey Wheeler. We're two of the sponsors of the rummage sale that's being held to raise money for Sleepyside Hospital. We were wondering if you have any secondhand items you'd like to contribute."

To the girls' surprise, the woman threw back her head and laughed. "I'd say you've come to the right place," she told them, opening the screen door. "Come right in.

"My name is Mrs. Manning, by the way," the woman said as she led the way to her basement.

"You see?" the woman asked, standing on the bottom step and gesturing at the most crowded jumble the girls had ever seen. "I'm something of a collector. I've been meaning to get rid of some of this junk —excuse me, secondhand merchandise—for quite a while. This is just the opportunity I've been waiting for, obviously.

"Now, this box," she said, "contains baby clothes. They're all in quite good condition, as I recall. But would you believe it, my youngest child is now in college?" She shook her head, smiling at the joke she'd just told on herself.

"These are some of my auction purchases over here. Anything that's being sold for a dollar or two always seems like such a bargain—until I get it home and have to decide what to do with it," she continued.

"What's that?" Trixie asked, pointing at the object the woman now held in her hand.

"Ah!" the woman exclaimed fondly. "This is a genuine collector's item. It's an antique canteen. It's a canvas bag, you see, with a rope handle, so it could be hung over a saddlehorn. Here's the spout, here. It still has the original cork in it, with a string attaching the cork to the bag so it won't get lost."

"I thought a canteen was something to hold water," Trixie said.

"It is," the woman told her.

"But wouldn't a canvas canteen leak?" Trixie asked.

"Yes, indeed. That's the whole point!" The woman threw back her head and laughed again at the girls' bewildered expressions. "It doesn't leak very much, because the fibers swell when they get wet. But it does leak a little bit. And the water that leaks through evaporates, and the evaporation acts as a coolant. The water never gets warm, even if it's exposed to the sun for hours at a time."

"How clever!" Honey exclaimed.

"Isn't it?" the woman agreed. "Of course, now we have all those insulated plastic jugs, which are really better. But these were still being used when I was a little girl. That's why I couldn't resist buying this thing at that auction. It was only a dollar."

She held the bag up by the rope handle. "I thought it would look rather interesting hanging on a wall. But I never found quite the right spot for it, so it wound up down here with all the rest of these things."

"Could I ask what that is?" Honey said, pointing.

"Oh, now, that's a very interesting item," the woman said. "You, of course, can't remember anything further back than the automatic washer. But there was a time—not that long ago, either— when women used to wash everything by hand, in big metal tubs. This is the washstand that held the tubs. You see, it's just a wooden frame. One tub, with soapy water, goes here. The other tub, with clear rinse water, goes here. And rising up between them is a wringer. The woman who was washing fed all the clothes through the wringer to get as much soapy water out of them as possible. See? This crank turns the rollers."

"The wringer still works!" Trixie said.

"Well, as I said, these washstands were in use not too terribly long ago." She gave the wringer a final turn. "Not as efficient as the spin cycle on your mother's washing machine, I'm sure, but it did the job in those days.

"The reason I bought this was that a friend of mine has one she used as a stand for her stereo. The turntable goes on this side, and the receiver goes over here. It's very clever, and quite a conversation piece. Unfortunately," the woman added ruefully, "my husband hated the idea. So here it sits."

"Someone at the rummage sale would probably love to have it," Honey said politely. "We could put a sign on it explaining the stereo-stand idea."

The woman nodded her head. "Yes, that would be wise. It would probably bring a few dollars more if someone knew there was a use for it."

She stood for a moment, looking around her at her accumulated belongings. "I don't have to have everything ready right this minute, do I?"

"Oh, no," Trixie said hurriedly. "In fact, it wouldn't do much good if you did. You see, we're on foot. We'll just take down your address and come back later with a station wagon."

"I'll have everything ready by seven o'clock this evening," the woman said firmly.

"Oh, you can have a few days, if you like," Honey suggested.

"Seven o'clock this evening," the woman repeated. "I'm feeling energetic about the idea right now, so right now is when I'd better carry it out."

"We'll be back at seven," Trixie promised.

"Yippee!" Trixie shouted when they were back on the sidewalk. "We hit the jackpot there, Honey! I bet we've taken an early lead in the contest."

"I'm not so sure," Honey told her. "That woman *may* have lots to donate. Or she may decide she can't bear to part with anything. You never can tell with a collector like that. Meantime, we spent almost half an hour talking to her. At that rate, we'll hit about eight houses before it's time for Jim to pick us up."

Trixie wrinkled her nose. "You're right, as usual. Those things were awfully interesting, though, weren't they?"

Honey nodded. "But let's just remember that we'll spend plenty of time with those interesting donations, putting prices on them and setting them out for the sale. We don't have to spend a lot of time on them now."

"Right," Trixie said emphatically. "Now, let's go on to the next house."

But at the next house, nobody was home. At the one after that, the man who answered the doorbell said, rather coldly, that he had nothing at all to contribute.

Trixie sighed as the girls walked up to the next house. "I guess our first stop was just beginner's luck. I'm beginning to wonder if we'll get any more donations at all."

"Why, yes," Honey said in exaggerated tones of agreement. "It's been all of five minutes since we've found even one little donation. I don't blame you for being worried."

Trixie giggled. "You know, as much as I hate having Beatrix for my real name, I think it could have been a lot worse. My parents could have named me 'Patience!'"

Both girls were still giggling when a short, stout woman answered the door at the next house.

This time it was Honey who introduced herself and Trixie and explained the reason for their visit.

"Oh, dear," the woman said breathlessly. "Oh, dear, it's such a worthy cause, and I just can't think of anything— Oh! Wait just a moment! Will you accept books?"

"Oh, yes!" Trixie said. "I'm sure that books would sell very well."

The woman's face brightened. "Then I do have something to donate. My children are both in college now, and the last time they were home for vacation, they sorted through all their books and set aside the ones they decided they'd outgrown. They're all in a box downstairs. Come right this way."

"We can't take them right now—" Trixie began. She turned to Honey helplessly as the woman continued down the stairs.

"We have to follow her," Honey whispered. "It would be rude not to. But let's not get involved in a long conversation."

"No, of course not," Trixie said.

"Well, here they are," the woman said, puffing as she pulled the large box out of the closet. She opened the box and began holding up some of the books. "These were my children's favorites. That's why they bought their own copies, instead of just taking them out of the library."

"Look!" Trixie exclaimed. "There's a Lucy Radcliffe novel!"

"Oh, yes, Lucy Radcliffe," the woman said fondly. "She was my daughter's special favorite. I don't think there was a single Lucy Radcliffe novel that Beverly didn't read."

"Those are my favorite books, too," Trixie said. "Lucy travels all over the world, and she's always uncovering spy rings and finding herself in terrible danger."

"That's just how Beverly used to describe the books," the woman said. "And she'd get that same starry look in her eyes."

"You can imagine how thrilled I was when I actually got to meet the author," Trixie said.

"You *met* the author?" the woman said in astonishment. "Oh, you must tell me what she's like. Bev would never forgive me if I didn't ask."

"Actually, *she's* a *he*," Trixie said. "The author's name is Mr. Appleton, and he's a very nice, quiet man, although for a while we *did* think he was a murderer. We met him at a resort in the Catskills, where we'd gone to—"

Honey Wheeler cleared her throat. "We'd love to tell you the entire story sometime. Maybe you could come to the rummage sale and chat with us there. Right now, though, we have to get going. If you'll just set a time, my brother will come around with our station wagon to collect these books."

"Of course, of course. I mustn't keep you. I plan to go to the rummage sale, so I can talk more with you then," the woman said. "Tell your brother he can drop by for the books anytime tonight."

The girls said their thank-you's and left. On the front step, Honey turned to Trixie with a stern look on her face. "I thought you said no more long conversations," she said accusingly.

Trixie was crestfallen. "I got carried away. From now on I won't say a word more than I have to." She went a few steps down the walk, then froze in her tracks. "Yipes!" she yelled. "With all I've been saying that I *didn't* have to, I haven't been saying what I *did* have to!"

100

Honey looked at her best friend in puzzlement. "We've explained we're collecting for the rummage sale, and we've told the people Jim will come to pick up the donations later on today. What more is there that we have to say?"

"Honey, you're forgetting why we're here. I mean, the *other* reason we're here. I mean, the reason we're *right* here. Oh, I mean the miser," she finished in exasperation. "I was going to drop that word into the conversation at every house we went to, to see if anyone reacted to it."

"That's right," Honey said. "Oh, why can't I keep more than one thing in my mind at a time? When I was worried about the stranger, I forgot about the rummage sale. Now I'm worried about getting the most donations for the rummage sale, so I forgot all about the stranger."

"I did the same thing," Trixie said sadly. Then she brightened. "Well, I certainly don't think either of the two women we've talked to so far had anything to hide. They certainly didn't act like it. But I'll ride along with Jim tonight when he comes back, just in case. I can work the word *miser* in then. For now, we'll just remind ourselves to remember at the other houses we go to."

At the next house, the door was opened by a pretty, blond-haired woman. "Wonderful!" she exclaimed when the girls told her about the rummage sale.

"My husband and I have been married just a few months, but we both had our own apartments for several years before that. That means we have two of everything, from toasters to vacuum cleaners. Actually, we have *three* of some things, because of the wedding gifts we received. This rummáge sale will give us a chance to contribute something to our new hometown *and* weed out our belongings."

"Well, if you've accumulated all those things, I guess you must not be *misers*," Trixie said, accenting the last word clumsily.

The woman looked at her curiously. "No, I guess we must not be," she said, obviously bewildered at the turn the conversation had taken.

"Would tomorrow evening be a convenient time for us to pick up your donation?" Honey said hastily.

"Yes, that would be fine," the woman said. The confused look was still on her face when she closed the door.

"Really, Trixie," Honey said as they walked to the next house, "I think you'll have to be more subtle than that if you're going to work in the word *miser*. People will think we're crazy and refuse to give us anything."

"Well, *you* mention the miser next time, then," Trixie retorted.

A little girl of about Bobby's age opened the door of the next house.

"Hi," Trixie said cheerfully. "Is your mom home?"

The little girl nodded solemnly. "We're all home," she said. "We don't get to go out and play or anything."

Trixie frowned. "Have you been sick?" she asked.

The little girl shook her head, still unsmiling. "We're okay. We just don't get to go out, that's all. My mother—"

The little girl was interrupted by a haggard-looking young woman. "Can I help you?" she asked sharply.

Trixie looked at Honey, who began the now-familiar introduction. While Honey spoke, the little girl ducked through the doorway and plopped on the lawn, where she began hunting, Trixie supposed, for a four-leaf clover.

"I'm sorry," the woman said more politely than before. "We just moved to Sleepyside. We weeded out our belongings quite thoroughly before we moved, so we really have nothing left to donate."

"I understand," Honey said tactfully. "I moved to Sleepyside not so long ago, myself. I remember how my mother tried to weed out our things, so that it would be easier to pack. But Daddy kept putting everything back where it had been. Mother got so mad, she told him he was a 'regular old miser.' "

Honey had worked the word into her conversation so skillfully that even Trixie was surprised to hear it.

But the woman's reaction was more noticeable than her own. She stiffened and turned her attention to the child playing on the lawn. "Melissa! You come inside this instant!"

The little girl jumped up and ducked back into the house.

"We really have nothing to contribute," the woman said, her voice harsh once again.

Before the two girls could say another word, the door slammed shut.

A Hard Night's Work • 6

"DID YOU SEE THAT?" Trixie whispered excitedly as they started down the walk.

"How could I miss it?" Honey answered softly. "The poor woman looked as if she'd been stung."

"She must be connected with the stranger in some way," Trixie said.

"I suppose so," Honey replied.

"You *suppose* so? What other explanation is there?" Trixie demanded.

"I don't know, but I'm sure if we told Jim and Brian what just happened, *they'd* think of something. Maybe it was my whole story that offended the woman. Maybe she moved here to get away from a husband who really *was* a miser," Honey said. "Maybe she has nothing to donate to the sale because he wouldn't let her take anything along. Maybe she was willing to leave it all behind just to get away from him."

"What about what her little girl said about not being allowed outside? How does that fit into your theory?" Trixie asked.

"Maybe her husband was so awful that she ran away, without telling him where she was going. Maybe she's hiding the children from him," Honey answered.

"Do you really believe that, Honey Wheeler?" Trixie demanded.

"No," Honey said meekly. "You know I almost always agree with your theories. That is, I agree with them until we tell them to Jim and Brian and Mart and they start picking them apart. The theory about that woman's having run away is just what I can imagine one of the boys saying."

"Well, I think the theories they invent to show me how farfetched mine are, are more farfetched than mine are, sometimes. Oh, you know what I mean!" Trixie said.

"Okay," Honey responded, without even a smile at Trixie's twisted sentence, "let's say this woman *is* somehow connected with the hit-and-run victim. What can we do about it?"

"Why, we can go right back to the house and tell her there's an unidentified man at Sleepyside Hospital who might be someone she knows," Trixie said.

"But what if she *is* running away from someone?" Honey asked. "We'll scare the daylights out of her if we say that, and we won't have the man's name or anything else to help her decide if she really *does* know him."

"Yes, but what if he's someone she cares about?" Trixie countered. "Do you think she's any less scared waiting around day after day in a strange town not knowing what happened to him or where he is or anything?"

Honey sighed. "That's true, too. Still, you know what Jim and Brian would say: 'Two perfect strangers went to a woman's door asking for donations to a rummage sale. One of them told a long, rambling story that happened to have the word 'miser' in it. The woman was startled by the word, or maybe by the story, or maybe just because some total stranger seemed to be telling her whole life story on her doorstep. She went inside and closed the door. It isn't enough for us to go getting involved in somebody's life.' "

"Now you sound like the stranger," Trixie said, "talking about not getting involved."

"It isn't the same thing," Honey protested. "That

man made it sound as though we shouldn't get involved with people because of what they might do to us. I'm thinking about what we might do to that woman if we butt in with no more information than we have. We might frighten her, scare her out of town, even put her life in danger, just because of the way we imagine she reacted to a single word."

"You don't sound like the stranger anymore," Trixie said. "You sound exactly like Jim now. Why did we have to find you such a cautious, sensible brother?"

"I think he's a perfectly perfect brother," Honey said. "You think he's pretty special, too."

Trixie blushed. The special feelings she had for Jim were ones she tried to keep to herself. "Well, what are we going to do?" she asked, partly to change the subject.

"It seems to me that Sergeant Molinson's advice about the hit and run applies just as well here," Honey said. "We have to wait until the victim is identified. Only then can we start looking for connections. In the meantime, we'd better hurry and get a lot more donations in the time we have left before Jim picks us up. Otherwise, we'll be way behind in the contest."

"All right," Trixie said reluctantly. "I guess it won't do any good to double my troubles by winding up Mart's temporary slave."

The girls' luck for the rest of the afternoon was neither good nor bad. They found no one home at a few houses, they were refused entry at some houses, and they were promised donations at several more.

When the station wagon picked them up at five o'clock, Jim, Mart, Dan, and Di were all inside, eager to discuss their afternoon's adventures.

"How did you two do?" Di Lynch asked as the girls got into the wagon.

"Pretty well, I think," Trixie answered. "The first house we went to was definitely the best. The woman who lives there is a regular rummage collector, and she had stories to tell about each thing. It took us ages and ages to get out of her basement, but she promised to have everything ready to pick up this evening."

"Then, at another house," Honey put in, "Trixie had a story of her own to tell. We didn't get out of there for ages, either."

"There are two kinds of people in the world, I've decided," Jim said. "There are those who like to talk to strangers and those who don't."

His words reminded Trixie of the haggard woman who had reacted so violently to the word *miser*. She frowned, wanting to tell the other Bob-Whites about their conversation with the woman, but not wanting to, at the same time.

Trixie turned to look at Honey. Her best friend,

also frowning, shook her head almost imperceptibly. She, too, was unwilling to have yet another theory dismantled.

Completely oblivious to Trixie and Honey's wordless exchange, Mart announced, "Our most commodious consignment far outshines yours; therefore I conclude that our total intake is also greater."

"Oh, Mart, let me tell them about it, please!" Di Lynch pleaded. Di was usually impressed with Mart's enormous vocabulary, but in this case, it seemed, the story was so good that she didn't want it delayed by translations.

"Go ahead, Di, please," Trixie said. "We'd love to hear you tell the story."

"Well," Di began, her violet eyes sparkling with excitement, "our big find, like yours, was at the very first house we went to. At first the woman who answered the door seemed sort of unfriendly. I felt my stomach sinking right down into my shoes, because I really don't enjoy going door to door like that, and finding somebody who wasn't very friendly right off the bat like that would have simply—"

"Di!" Trixie interrupted. "You're supposed to be giving us the shorter version, remember?"

Di put her fingers to her mouth. "I guess I was getting a little carried away," she said. "Anyway, it turned out that the woman wasn't really unfriendly.

She was just distracted because she had something else on her mind. When she finally heard what we were saying, that we wanted donations to the rummage sale, she got this big, bright smile on her face.

"You see, the reason she was so upset is that she's having a whole new houseful of furniture delivered tomorrow, and she couldn't figure out what she was going to do with what she has now!" Di clapped her hands together delightedly and bounced up and down on the car seat as she concluded her story.

"Are you saying that you got an entire houseful of furniture at your very first stop today?" Trixie asked, unwilling to believe what she'd just heard.

"Well, no, not exactly," Di said, with an impish grin. "The woman's dining room set was an antique, so she decided to keep that. All we got was the couch and two chairs, a coffee table, and two end tables from the living room; a double bed and two sets of twin beds, all with matching dressers and chests of drawers and night tables, of course, and—"

"Stop! Stop!" Trixie shouted. "I can't stand it. With every single item you're listing, I'm hearing the slow, heavy ticking of a clock—a clock that will count out the five hours of slavery that is my fate." Trixie dramatically clutched her hands to her heart and fell back against the car seat, a look of exaggerated despair on her face.

Di beamed triumphantly, and she slipped her arm

through Mart's. "I guess we're the winning team," she told him.

"This contest can't be won in a day," Jim muttered. "Don't count your servants before they're hatched, to mangle an ancient proverb."

"There is veracity in that ancient adage," Mart said dreamily. "And yet it is with difficulty that I banish pleasant visions from my imagination. Even yet, I seem to see sandy curls dripping with perspiration as the snub-nosed cherub whom they adorn pushes a lawn mower . . . polishes storm windows until they glisten . . . scrubs—"

"Snub-nosed!" Trixie shrieked. The insult had kept her from hearing the veiled threats that came after it. "Your nose isn't exactly a thing of beauty, Mart Belden! I just wish the contest today had been for finding clues instead of bedroom sets. Then we'd see who's the clear winner!" She regretted her outburst immediately, but it was too late to call the words back.

"What's this about clues?" Jim asked.

"Nothing," Trixie said sullenly.

"Come on, Trixie," Jim said. "As I recall, the Bob-Whites are supposed to be loyal to one another."

"If you and Brian and Mart were loyal to Honey and me, you wouldn't always tear apart everything we say," Trixie said, on the verge of tears as her worries about losing to Mart in the contest combined with her rapidly surfacing anger. "Whenever Honey and I *do* tell you what we know, you try to tell us we don't really know it at all. So this time, we're not going to tell you at all."

"You're miffed because nobody flew into action when you proposed that the hit and run wasn't accidental," Jim guessed. "All right, I don't blame you. It isn't pleasant to have someone doubt what our reason tells us. I guess I don't even blame you for not wanting to risk having that happen again. If you don't want to tell us your theory, that's all right."

As Jim spoke, he turned the station wagon into the driveway of Crabapple Farm. He put the car in park and turned around in the seat, looking Trixie directly in the eye as he continued: "If you decide to *do* something about your theory without telling anyone else, that is *not* all right. If you get into trouble, someone else had better know enough about what's going on to help you out of it. Understand?"

Trixie sat motionless, frozen by Jim's sincere gaze. Finally she looked down at her hands in her lap and nodded.

"We'd already decided not to do anything about our theory until we have more information, Jim," Honey said.

"Okay," Jim said. "Now, everybody give me your lists of donors so I can make the pickup rounds tonight with the wagon."

Mart and Honey handed over their lists. Trixie continued to stare at her hands, trying to convince herself that Jim had lectured her out of concern for her safety. It was true, she had to admit, that she and Honey had both had close calls when they plunged into action without telling anybody about it. Jim had a point, she finally concluded.

"C-Could I ride along tonight when you go to pick up things for the sale?" she asked timidly.

Jim grinned at her. "Sure can," he said. "I can't think of anyone else I'd rather be with tonight. Remember, though, that we're in for a lot of hard work and not a relaxing movie," he warned her with a mock grimace.

Trixie felt the knot in her stomach begin to relax. It was important, she knew, that she not allow herself to avoid Jim, letting her anger grow and turning his concerned warning into an unfeeling lecture in her mind.

It was important, too, that she get another look at the house on Glenwood Avenue where the troubled woman and the little blond girl seemed to be holding themselves captive.

The Beldens' dinner-hour conversation was completely taken up with talk of the rummage sale.

The Model A had pulled into the Belden driveway shortly after the station wagon had pulled out of it.

Brian, like the other Bob-Whites, had a mixture of success and failure to report.

"If we could get points toward winning the contest for drawing the most *people* to the sale, I'd win hands down," he said. "Everybody had questions about the car I was driving, and when I said there was going to be an antique car show along with the rummage sale, everyone said they'd be there for sure."

Brian chuckled to himself. "The other way for me to be a clear winner would be to add in the number of times someone pulled up alongside me at a stop sign and yelled, 'Get a horse!' That happened about five hundred and sixty-one times."

"It's sort of unfair that you have to make your rounds alone," Trixie said sympathetically.

"Oh, don't take my grousing seriously," Brian told her. "I actually did pretty well on donations to the sale, too. *My* jackpot was a woman who had held a rummage sale of her own—on the day of the biggest rainstorm all season! Nobody came to her sale, so she has lots of stuff boxed up in the basement, all neatly folded and with the price tags still in place."

"Gleeps, Brian! That brings up a problem I hadn't even thought of: What are we going to do with the things that don't sell?" Trixie asked.

"We'll bundle them up and give them to charity,"

Brian said. "One way or another, everything people donate will contribute to a worthy cause."

"Doesn't that make you feel good?" Trixie asked, eyes sparkling. "I just don't understand people who don't want to get involved."

"Like our stranger, you mean?" Brian asked his sister. "I don't think most people start out that way. Sometimes, though, if a person gets hurt by another person, that one tragic experience is enough to make him or her decide that *people* mean *pain*."

"People must miss out on an awful lot when they decide to keep everyone else from getting involved with them," Trixie said.

"They avoid both pain and pleasure that way," Helen Belden observed.

"They avoid stern lectures from people who care about them, too," Mart said pointedly.

"I get the message," Trixie said. "In fact, I sent myself that same message while we were still in the car." She stood up and began to clear the table. "I think that made me the clear winner today, no matter who's ahead in the contest." She nodded archly at Mart and stalked into the kitchen.

Just as the last of the dishes were dried and put away, the Bob-White station wagon pulled into the driveway. "Gotta go, Moms," Trixie said, drying her hands and tucking the dish towel onto the rack.

She ran out the back door and hopped into the car.

"You're full of energy after a long day," Jim observed as he backed out of the drive.

"I'm just eager to see what Mrs. Manning finally decided she could part with," Trixie said.

"I hope she doesn't let you down," Jim said.

"I don't think she will," Trixie replied. "She seemed like such a nice lady. Oh, speaking of nice ladies, there's one house I don't dare set foot in tonight. If I do, we won't get home until midnight." Briefly, Trixie told Jim about the woman who wanted to know all about the "real" Lucy Radcliffe.

Jim laughed at Trixie's imitation of the woman's breathless eagerness. "I agree. You'd better wait in the car while I go inside. Believe me, I won't even hint that I was in the Catskills with you when you met 'Lucy.'"

The two Bob-Whites rode the rest of the way in silence, and Trixie found her thoughts turning to the woman who Trixie was sure was connected somehow with the hit-and-run victim. When Jim turned the station wagon onto the first block Trixie and Honey had covered that afternoon, it was that house, not Mrs. Manning's, that Trixie strained to see.

"Where do we start?" Jim asked as he drove slowly down the block.

"What?" Trixie pulled her attention back to the

117

car. "Oh, Jim, I'm sorry. Mrs. Manning lives back on the corner. You can turn around in this driveway."

"And this driveway belongs to the house you'd *really* like to visit," Jim guessed.

Trixie flushed guiltily.

"You don't have to explain anything," Jim added hastily. "I told you that this afternoon, and I meant it." He paused for a moment in the driveway, staring at the house. "Just looking at it, I'd say nobody lived there at all. The drapes are all shut tight. There are no lights showing anywhere. There are no trikes or bikes or balls or bats lying out on the lawn."

"That's just what I was thinking, Jim," Trixie told him. "I was also remembering that those drapes were closed this afternoon, too. Think how gloomy it must be inside! That poor little girl!"

Jim looked at Trixie curiously, but, true to his word, he didn't ask any questions. Putting the car in reverse, he backed out of the driveway. "We want the house on the corner, you said?"

Mrs. Manning had the door open before the Bob-Whites were out of the car. "You're going to be so proud of me!" she called as they came up the walk. "I was very firm with myself. 'Out it goes!' I said whenever I felt myself wanting to hold on to something."

She led them to the basement and pointed at a huge pile in one corner. "Out it goes!" she repeated, flinging one arm out in a gesture of banishment.

"Okay—out it goes," Jim agreed as he walked toward the pile. He picked up a box from which a piece of weathered wood protruded.

"Now, that's a doubletree," Mrs. Manning said, reaching out and putting a hand on the piece of wood. "It was originally used to yoke a pair of horses together, but I thought it would be lovely for hanging a hooked rug or an old quilt on the wall. I do wish I had a wall big enough." She let go of the doubletree reluctantly, and Jim carried the box out of the basement.

Trixie picked up an open box filled with picture frames.

"Those were a real bargain," Mrs. Manning told her. "The whole box went at auction for just two dollars. Some of them are really lovely, and the cost of frames these days is truly out of sight! Of course, you have to have just the right pictures to go in them, and since they're so old, some of the sizes are rather odd."

"I'm sure someone will be delighted to find them," Trixie said politely.

Trixie and Jim made several trips up the stairs, each time carrying something that Mrs. Manning had almost, but not quite, found the perfect use for.

119

When the corner of the basement was empty, the station wagon was almost full.

"I hope you don't have too much more to collect yet tonight," Mrs. Manning said.

"As a matter of fact, we do," Jim said. "We may have to make a trip home to drop things off. This is a bigger job than I'd figured, I'm afraid."

"Well, we can at least get that box of books in," Trixie said.

"Oh, is Glenda Maurer giving you the books her children sorted out over vacation?" Mrs. Manning asked.

"Why, yes—that is, I guess it's Mrs. Maurer. She lives in the third house down," Trixie said.

Mrs. Manning nodded smugly. "That's Glenda. She'd mentioned just last week that she had to get around to calling someone about those books. Your timing was perfect there, too."

"This must be quite a close-knit neighborhood," Jim said.

"Oh, yes," Mrs. Manning told him. "Most of us have lived here for years and years. We all have children about the same ages, and our children played together while they were growing up. We took turns baby-sitting, chairing the PTA—that sort of thing."

"There's one house that doesn't seem to fit that pattern," Jim said.

"There are two I can think of that don't, actually," Mrs. Manning corrected him. "There are the Greens. They're a young couple who just moved in next to the Maurers. They're newlyweds, so they don't have much in common with us old folks. Still, they're very nice young people.

"And then there are the Greens' neighbors." Mrs. Manning's tone changed to one of disapproval. "Of course, they may be nice, too, for all I know. But they certainly do keep to themselves. The drapes are pulled day and night. I *never* see anyone coming or going. In fact, I don't even know exactly how many people live there. It's all very mysterious, I must say."

"Well, I guess there's one family like that in every neighborhood," Jim said casually. "Thank you very much for your donation, Mrs. Manning," he added as he and Trixie got in the car. "I hope we'll see you at the sale."

"I'd love to come, but I'm not sure I dare. I might buy more than I got rid of!" Laughing at her own foolishness, Mrs. Manning waved good-bye and went back into the house.

"Well, the next stop is Mrs. Maurer's house, I guess," Jim said as he turned the key in the ignition.

Trixie looked at him appreciatively. Jim had made a point of getting more information about the house Trixie was curious about. But, still true to his word, he wasn't going to force Trixie to confide her theory.

That was comforting. So was the fact that Mrs. Manning's thoughts about the Greens' neighbors confirmed Trixie's own. "It's all very mysterious, I must say," Mrs. Manning had said.

I must say so, too, Trixie thought.

A Visit With the Victim • 7

FOR THE NEXT THREE HOURS, however, Trixie was too hard-worked to think of the mystery. She and Jim carried load after load from people's houses to the station wagon. They made three trips back to the clubhouse to deposit the donations they'd collected.

By ten o'clock, when the last stop was made, they were red-faced and exhausted. Jim was concerned. "This is getting out of hand," he said. "Our original plan for the rummage sale was just to put up some posters and wait for people to call us. Now we're going door to door, and that means a lot more donations and a lot more pickups. I don't know if we're going to be able to handle it."

"But we can't just abandon the rummage sale," Trixie wailed.

"I'm not suggesting that," Jim told her. "I'm saying that we have to make some changes in our way of handling the rummage sale."

"What kind of changes?" Trixie asked.

"For one thing, when we go door to door from now on, let's at least ask people whether they'd be willing to drop their donations off. If they seem at all reluctant, we can volunteer to pick things up. We don't want to discourage donations, after all. I think a lot of people would be willing to help out, though."

"That would save a lot of work, all right," Trixie admitted. "Oh, but Jim, we can't tell all those people where our clubhouse is! It's supposed to be a secret!"

Jim nodded. "I thought of that, too," he said. "Actually, what I thought of is the fact that the clubhouse won't begin to hold all the things we're collecting. What about Mart's entire houseful of furniture? The clubhouse won't even hold a spare couch now, let alone all the things Di was listing this afternoon."

"Gleeps, I forgot about that, too. What are we going to do, Jim?" Trixie asked despairingly.

"Tomorrow, we'll start looking for another place to keep the donations," Jim replied. "It should be someplace that's conveniently located, big enough to store all the items we collect, and open enough hours so that donors can drop things off more or less at their convenience. Spread the word to Brian and Mart when you get home. Tell your parents, too. The more people we have trying to think of a place, the better our chances are of coming up with something. We need a good idea, but fast!"

"I'll alert my family," Trixie promised, stifling a yawn. "Anyway, we only have one more load to unload tonight."

"Correction," Jim said firmly. "We have no more loads to unload tonight. I'm about to drop, and you look as though you are, too. It won't hurt these things to stay locked in the car overnight. Besides, if we're going to find a new place to store our donations tomorrow, it would be silly to move them into the clubhouse tonight."

"Sounds good to me," Trixie told him gratefully. "Even if it weren't a perfectly perfect idea, as Honey would say, I'm much too tired to argue."

When Jim pulled into the driveway of Crabapple Farm, Trixie barely had the strength to open the car door, wave goodnight to Jim, and stagger directly to bed.

At eight o'clock the next morning, Mrs. Belden knocked on the door to Trixie's room and called,

"Better get up. You're due at the hospital in less than an hour."

Trixie sat up in bed and raised her arms over her head, then halted in midstretch as her stiff muscles complained. She groaned and dropped back against the pillows, remembering the umpteen trips from people's basements to the Bob-White wagon she'd made the night before.

"At least, there's no chance of forgetting to tell my family that we need a new plan for collecting donations," Trixie told herself. "Every movement I make all day will remind me of it."

She pulled herself out of bed, dressed slowly, and went downstairs to breakfast.

"Good morning, Trixie," Brian said, looking up from his bacon and eggs as his sister slid into her place at the table. "How did everything go last night?"

Trixie related the events of the previous evening and told her family about Jim's directive regarding the collection plan.

"Do you think people could take their things directly to the school gymnasium, since that's where the sale will be held?" Brian asked.

Mr. Belden shook his head. "I doubt it, Brian. A custodian would have to be on duty every day at the school. Paying for his time would eat up most of the proceeds from your sale. There's bound to be some other place in town that meets the requirements. We'll all give it some thought and see what we can come up with."

"I don't think I'll think of anything," Trixie said foggily. "I think I'm too tired to think."

"A circumstance that is not as inconceivable as you would have us suppose," Mart teased.

Trixie was too weary even to rise to the bait her brother offered. "I hope I'm assigned some easy duties today at the hospital. I *might* be able to read a storybook to a youngster—if the pages aren't too heavy to turn."

"Don't forget to find out whatever you can about the hit-and-run victim," Brian told her.

"I'm not too tired to remember that," Trixie assured him. "I'll make a full report when I get home this afternoon."

"In return for that, and for your hard work last night, I'm prepared to offer you a ride to the hospital in the vehicle of your choice," Brian said. "Would you prefer the Model A or my jalopy?"

Trixie giggled. "Some choice," she teased. "I'll take whichever one is most *un*likely to break down on the way!"

"Let's make it the jalopy, then," Brian said with a grin. "It isn't really less likely to break down, but *I'm* more likely to know what to do when it does. Are you ready, Trix?"

His sister drained the last of her orange juice and pushed back her chair. "I'm as ready as I'll ever be," she said.

At the hospital, Trixie reported to the director of volunteers, Ms. Lee, who looked at the young Volunteen critically. "We have patients who look healthier than you do, Trixie," she said. "Are you feeling all right?"

Trixie shook her head ruefully and told Ms. Lee about her hard work the night before.

"The hospital wants volunteers, not more patients," Ms. Lee chided gently when Trixie had finished. "I think you'd better take it easy today."

"I couldn't agree with you more," Trixie said gratefully.

"Why don't you go to the children's ward and read stories for a while?" Ms. Lee said. "Or is there something else you'd rather do?"

"There is one thing," Trixie said. She told Ms. Lee about her involvement with the hit-and-run victim who had been brought in two nights before. "I'd like to find out whatever I can about his condition," she concluded.

"Of course," Ms. Lee said. "In fact, I think it might be very helpful to us if you visit him. He's been conscious since early this morning, but he's refused to say a word to anyone. We still don't know his name or anything about him. Maybe he'll talk to you, since you helped to save his life the other night. You might be able to cheer him up, too, and that would undoubtedly aid in his recovery."

Trixie smiled at Ms. Lee. "It would aid in mine, too. Thanks!"

Trixie went to the stranger's room and knocked on the open door before she entered. When she walked into the room, she found him lying in bed, his head swathed in bandages.

The man stared at her hostilely. "What do you want?" he growled.

"I'm Trixie Belden," she told him. "My friends and I are wondering how you're doing."

"What friends?" the man demanded. "How do you know me? How did you know I was here?"

"Don't you remember?" Trixie asked. "The night of your accident—"

"If I remembered, I wouldn't have asked," the man said gruffly.

"Oh," Trixie said, looking at the white bandages wrapped around the stranger's head. She remembered Juliana Maasden, who had also been a hit-and-run victim. After the accident, Juliana had been unable to remember anything, even her own name. That sometimes happened with head injuries, the doctor had told the Bob-Whites.

"Right before your accident, you stopped to help

us with a stalled car—a Model A. Then you—We—"
Trixie searched for the right word. "We were there
when it—"

"You saw me get run over, you mean?" the man
asked.

Trixie nodded dumbly.

"They told me about you young people," the man
said. "Apparently you saved my life by keeping me
warm with your jackets and calling an ambulance
and waiting till it came."

"Well, we've been sort of feeling as though we'd
endangered your life," Trixie confessed. "I mean, if
you hadn't stopped to help us. . . ."

"That was my decision, not yours," the man said
coldly. "It was a Model A, you said?"

Trixie nodded. "There was something wrong with
the carburetor. You fixed it right away."

The man leaned back against his pillows and
stared at the ceiling. "I had a Model A once," he
said. "I bought it for fifty dollars back when they
were used cars, not antiques. I held it together with
chewing gum and baling wire for a year. I got to
know that car inside and out. It's what got me
started with—" The man broke off abruptly and
darted a nervous look at Trixie. "Anyway, it's not
surprising that I still remembered how to get one
started."

"It's a good thing you did," Trixie told him. "We

all feel as though we might still be sitting there in a stalled car if it hadn't been for you."

"How did you kids get your hands on a Model A, anyway?" the man asked. "They're pretty rare these days."

"It really isn't our Model A," Trixie explained. "It's a donation for the rummage sale we're sponsoring to benefit the hospital. Mr. Burnside, who owns the lumberyard here in Sleepyside, donated it. He thought we could attract more attention to the sale if we drove the car around town for a few days ahead of time."

"It ought to do that, all right," the stranger agreed. "It ought to fetch a lot of money for the hospital, too."

"Isn't it wonderful? We couldn't believe our luck when Mr. Burnside decided to donate the Model A," Trixie exulted. "I still don't understand how he can part with it, but he bought an old Stanley Steamer, and he likes that even better, I guess."

"A Stanley!" the stranger exclaimed. The harsh look on his face was replaced by a thoughtful smile. "No transmission, infinite throttle. What a machine! Nobody ever did find out how fast one could go. The Stanley was designed by a couple of twin brothers, F.E. and F.O. Stanley. Before they got interested in cars, they were already successful inventors. They were the first to mass-produce violins, for one thing.

They also developed the first packaged photographic negatives.

"Then, back in eighteen ninety-seven, they went to a county fair and watched a demonstration of a new 'horseless carriage.' The thing broke down before it made a single lap around the racetrack at the fairgrounds. The Stanleys decided they could do better—and they did!

"They had a great time doing it, too. One of their favorite tricks was to take off down the road a few minutes apart in matching cars. A policeman would flag down the first brother to give him a lecture about not going too fast in that newfangled contraption, then stop in midsentence when he saw what looked like the exact same man going by in the exact same car!"

Trixie laughed as she imagined the startled look on the policeman's face. "They sound as if they would have been interesting men to know," she said. "I always thought of inventors as boring, humorless men."

The injured man shot Trixie a strange look. "Oh, you did, did you? Well, the Stanley brothers, at least, were anything but that."

"What finally happened to them?" Trixie asked.

The stranger's face darkened again. "They got themselves tangled up with the money men," he said. "If I were to generalize about inventors, I wouldn't say they were humorless, but I would say they're too doggoned trusting.

"In the Stanleys' case, a couple of hotshots started pestering them to sell the rights to the Steamer. F.E. and F.O. didn't want to do it, so they set what they thought was an astronomical price—two hundred and fifty thousand dollars. The hotshots wrote out a check, and the Stanleys were out of business. They got back together later on, but by that time their best inventing days were over."

"That's terrible!" Trixie said indignantly. "Why, just think what two brilliant men like that could have done. They might have come up with a car that would go hundreds of miles on a gallon of gas and not pollute the air at all and—and all kinds of things!"

"They might have, at that," the man told her. "In some ways, the Stanley was the best car ever designed. But it did have problems. The water tanks used to freeze up in the winter, and after people got used to the idea of a horseless carriage, they wanted one that would get up and go right *now*, never mind the fact that they had been used to spending plenty of time hitching up a team of horses to a buggy. I bet the Stanleys could have solved those problems, if they hadn't been railroaded out of their own company."

Trixie looked at the stranger's bitter expression. *You'd almost think it had happened to him, instead*

133

of to the Stanleys, she thought. Aloud she said, "You told us the other night that cars were your passion. I can certainly see now how true that is."

The stranger's expression darkened even more. "I told you that, did I? Just what else did I say?"

"N-Nothing," Trixie said, taken aback by the man's scowl. "Well, you did ask us how to get to Glenwood Avenue."

"Glenwood Avenue," the man repeated. "Did I give an address on Glenwood Avenue?"

Trixie shook her head. Then she gasped as she realized the probable reason for the stranger's concern. "You don't remember where you were going that night, either, do you?" she guessed. "I should have thought of that. You see, I knew someone once who had amnesia after an accident like yours."

"Amnesia," the man repeated slowly. "Yeah, I guess that's what I have, all right. I don't remember anything about the last few days."

"Well, you mustn't worry about it," Trixie said. "I'm sure your memory will come back. Juliana— that's my friend who had amnesia—couldn't remember anything at all! But her memory came back eventually, and I'm sure yours will, too."

"Yes, I'm sure it will," the man said in an odd tone of voice.

"Anyway, there's a chance that you'll soon know what your name is, even if you don't remember it yourself. Sergeant Molinson told us he took a set of fingerprints from you while you were unconscious. He's running them through the FBI files. If you were a defense plant worker or a big executive or anything, your prints will be on file.''

Trixie carefully avoided mentioning that a criminal record would also be a reason for the FBI to have a set of fingerprints. But the stranger apparently thought of that possibility for himself. "So everybody's decided I'm a con, huh, because I didn't have a wad of credit cards in my pocket with my name all over them?"

"Nobody's decided—" Trixie began.

"Oh, I know how people's minds work. If you aren't a cookie-cutter image of everybody else, then you're dangerous. Why, I'm surprised you dare to be in the same room with me, young lady. I didn't come all wrapped up in a three-piece suit and tied with a bow. I don't even have references from my banker!"

"I don't—" Trixie began again.

"Never mind!" the stranger growled. "You're going to tell me you're not like that. *You* like people for themselves. Hogwash! You're like everyone else in the world, and I don't like any of you. Now, get out!"

The man's voice had risen to a frenzied shout, and Trixie was afraid that he might make himself sick if she didn't leave. She turned and made a hasty retreat from the room.

Out in the hall, Trixie leaned against a cool tiled wall and tried to collect her thoughts. The stranger obviously remembered *something*—something about the way he'd been treated by people in the past. She thought about what the stranger had said the night of the accident about not getting involved with people. She thought, too, about what her brother had said the day before about people who got hurt by other people and decided never to let it happen again.

Trixie also realized that she'd never got around to asking the stranger about the miser. *I wonder if the miser took something away from him and kept it. I wonder if that's why he hates people so.*

Then Trixie felt a jolt like an electric shock as another thought occurred to her. *I wonder if the miser is a woman!*

A Visit From a Vandal · 8

TRIXIE FINISHED HER MORNING at the hospital in a daze that was a combination of confusion from her conversation with the hit-and-run victim and fatigue. When Brian came for her, she was so lost in tired thought that she didn't notice the honking of the horn.

"Were you asleep on your feet all morning, or just for the past few minutes?" Brian asked teasingly as she climbed into the jalopy.

"Pretty much all morning," Trixie admitted sheepishly.

Brian laughed. "When we called Jim at ten o'clock, he'd just gotten out of bed. He managed to sound stiff and sore over the phone, if you can imagine such a thing."

"I don't have to imagine it," Trixie retorted. "It hurt me to turn the pages of a storybook. Picking up a telephone must have been agony!"

"Well, at least what we had to tell him was a balm to his troubled mind, if not to his aching muscles. It's news you'll be happy to hear, too," Brian said.

"What is it?" Trixie asked impatiently. "Oh, you've solved the problem of picking up the donations, haven't you? How? I mean, where? I mean, *what*—what's the solution?"

"I'd love to tell you, but I can't," Brian replied. "The brainstorm was actually Mart's, and he's quite proud of himself for thinking of it. He'd never forgive me if he didn't get to tell you about it himself. I promised him my lips are sealed until I get you home."

"Oh-h-h," Trixie moaned, sinking back against the seat of the car. "I thought you said this news was going to make me feel better. Listening to Mart gloat is the last thing I need today. He'll probably go right from his solution to his theory that he's a clear winner in the contest. Just thinking about working off five hours in Mart's service makes my muscles ache twice as much."

But to Trixie's surprise, Mart was downright modest about his solution. "It was nothing, really," he said as he helped himself to a heaping handful of potato chips to go with his mountainous sandwich. "I just reviewed the criteria in my mind: A place that was centrally located and open to the public; a place that had lots of room; and, finally, a place that was owned or operated by someone sympathetic to our cause. Naturally—"

"The lumberyard!" Trixie shouted. "Mr. Burnside is going to let us store the rummage sale donations in one of the warehouses at the lumberyard, isn't he?"

Mart's face immediately began to look like a thundercloud. "Must lucidity of speech result in forfeiture of the right to completion?" he asked sulkily.

Trixie was sincerely apologetic. "It's just that having to wait till we got home made me so curious, Mart. I'm sorry I jumped the gun. Tell me all about it."

"There really isn't anything more to tell," Mart said, refusing to be appeased. "It's clear now that any birdbrain would have come to the conclusion I did that the lumberyard was an ideal location. We simply called Mr. Burnside and almost before we had explained the problem, he'd volunteered one of his warehouses."

"We spent the rest of the morning driving back around the places that still had donations to be picked up," Brian added. "We explained that we were simply getting too many donations to handle alone and asked if they'd mind dropping their things off. Everyone who had a car and could carry things to it agreed to our plan. There were two elderly women who needed help, so we picked up their donations for them and took them over to Mr. Burnside's."

"It really is the perfect solution, Mart," Trixie said, "for now, anyway. We'll still have to make thousands of trips from the lumberyard to the school on the morning of the sale."

"Mr. Burnside came through for us there, too," Brian said. "He's lending us two pickup trucks, complete with drivers. They'll have everything transported in a couple of hours."

"It's all settled, then," Trixie said. "I'm glad some of the Bob-Whites managed to get problems cleared up this morning."

"In other words you failed to ascertain the condition of our friend the stranger," Mart guessed eagerly, hoping to snatch Trixie's news from her as she had just done from him.

"He feels better physically, but he's hos-hostile," Trixie replied, struggling on the "Mart" word. "I talked to him for quite a while."

"He couldn't have been too hostile, if he talked to you for 'quite a while,' " Helen Belden pointed out.

"He wasn't really hostile to *me*. He's angry at the world in general. He was the same way the night of the accident, helping us get the Model A started and

140

then telling us he never gets involved with people," Trixie explained.

"I wonder if he isn't just an old softy underneath," Brian mused. "Mr. Maypenny is like that. He pretends to be so gruff, but he'd really do almost anything if someone needed his help."

"That's true—about Mr. Maypenny, I mean," Trixie said. She smiled as she thought about the Wheelers' gamekeeper. The old man had lived on his tiny, pie-shaped piece of land since long before Mr. Wheeler had begun to buy up the land around it for a game preserve. Mr. Maypenny had stubbornly refused to sell, but he had agreed to work for almost no salary, patrolling the area in search of poachers, wounded animals, and forest fires. He had also agreed to take Dan Mangan on as an assistant, pretending to think of the boy only as a worker but actually giving him the first secure home he'd ever known.

"The stranger isn't like that, though," Trixie continued. "Mr. Maypenny's gruffness is more from force of habit. He's been alone so much that he just doesn't know how to talk to people. The stranger really seems angry about something."

"Speaking of force of habit, why are you still calling our friend 'the stranger'? After talking to him all morning, I'd think you'd at least know his name," Brian said.

"Well, I don't. I don't think he remembers it," Trixie told her brother.

"You don't think he remembers it," Brian repeated impatiently. "Why not?"

"He didn't remember me or the Model A or asking about Glenwood Avenue. I never came right out and asked his name, though," Trixie admitted lamely.

"It's probably a good thing you didn't come right out and ask him if he remembered his name," Brian told her. "Not knowing that was what bothered Juliana more than anything else."

Trixie nodded. "I remembered Juliana as soon as the stranger told me he didn't remember the accident. I felt sorry for him, because I remembered how awful Juliana felt about having amnesia. But I felt better when I remembered that Juliana finally remembered, after all. I told the stranger that, too."

"I hope he remembers your words of consolation," Brian said, barely suppressing a chuckle.

"Yes, he's bound to feel better if he remembers that I remembered Juliana's remembering," Trixie said, picking up on the joke.

"Don't forget to remember to remind him if he forgets," Mart added.

"*You* forget it!" Trixie retorted, clutching two fistfuls of sandy curls. "I'm so tired I might not remember my own name by dinner time!"

"Would you like us to pin a note to your shirt?"

Brian inquired. "We could write your name and address on it. That way, if you find yourself in some strange neighborhood requesting donations this afternoon, unable to remember who you are, you can be returned to Crabapple Farm."

"I think that's too much to ask of our potential donors," Mart said. "We'll merely request that our worn-out sibling be dropped off at the lumberyard with the rest of the rummage."

"Oh, no," Trixie groaned. "Don't tell me we're planning to spend the afternoon requesting donations again!"

"I, for one, will be more than happy to grant your supplication," Mart said. "I will not breathe a word of our intent, thus propelling myself, by default, into the lead in our contest."

"In this case, what I don't know *can* hurt me," Trixie said. "When do we leave?"

Brian checked his watch. "Jim should be here in the station wagon with Honey, Di, and Dan in about fifteen minutes."

With a loud sigh, Trixie got up from the table. "That's really swell. I'll even have time to change clothes." She turned and walked slowly up the stairs to her room.

Very grateful for Honey's friendship-in-action that afternoon, Trixie trudged along beside her friend dumbly, forcing herself to smile when someone opened a door in response to their knock. Honey did the rest, repeating their request for donations at house after house.

For a while, Trixie tried to keep the record of who pledged items to the sale, who was willing to drop off their things at the lumberyard, and who needed to have donations picked up. But she found herself transposing house numbers and forgetting, by the time they got to the sidewalk, which category the last donor belonged in. Finally, Honey had to take over the recording as well.

"Even if we don't lose the contest, I'm going to owe you five hours of slave labor," Trixie told Honey when the afternoon was over and they were waiting for the station wagon. "I might as well not have been along this afternoon, for all the help I was."

"Well, *I* wasn't along last night when *you* worked yourself to the bone," Honey reminded her. "I'd say we're just about even."

The teams, too, seemed to be even in the amount of donations that had been pledged, Trixie discovered when the Bob-Whites compared notes on the way home.

"I'm grateful for that," she told her friends. "But there's something I'm even more grateful for."

"What's that?" Jim asked as he turned the station wagon into the driveway of Crabapple Farm.

"I'm grateful that, as far as I'm concerned, this day is over!" Trixie said emphatically. She hoisted herself out of the car and gave a halfhearted wave before walking into the house.

True to her word, Trixie asked her mother's permission to skip dinner and went directly to her room. Although it was only a little past five o'clock and the sunshine was still pouring in through her windows, she pulled on her pajamas and crawled into bed.

When she awoke, the sun was shining, but the quality of the light had changed. Trixie lay still for a moment, feeling confused and trying to decipher the reasons for her confusion.

Gradually she realized that her early bedtime had thrown her routine out of kilter. "Did I just doze for a while, or did I sleep all night?" she asked herself. She raised her head to look at the alarm clock by her bed. "Eight o'clock," she read. She let her head fall back on the pillow while she tried groggily to figure out what *that* meant.

Trixie stretched every muscle in her body. Gradually she woke up, realizing that the stiffness that had plagued her the day before was almost gone this morning.

"It's a brand-new day," she said happily, sitting up and swinging her legs over the side of the bed.

It was only when she was sitting up that she became aware of the noise downstairs. Although the Belden household was often in an uproar at mealtimes or in the evening, mornings were usually very quiet at Crabapple Farm.

"Something must be wrong," Trixie said to herself. She pulled on her slippers and robe and ran downstairs.

In the kitchen, Brian Belden was shouting and waving his arms wildly. Mart was yelling, too, and Bobby, alarmed by Brian's being upset, was crying.

"What's going on?" Trixie shouted into the din.

Brian broke off in midsentence and waved toward the back door. "See for yourself," he barked.

Trixie walked outside and froze as her glance fell on the Model A. There was something strange-looking about the antique car, and immediately Trixie knew that the car was what was throwing her calm oldest brother into such an uproar.

She stared at the car, trying to decide what was different about it. "It's lower!" she exclaimed. She looked at the tires. They were all flat. "The signs are missing, too!" she added.

"They're there, all right," Brian said behind her. "They're lying broken on the ground beside the car. The tires are flat because they were slashed. And if you walk around to the front, you'll see that both the headlights are smashed."

146

Trixie's face was white under its spattering of freckles as she turned to look at her brother. "But why?"

Brian's jaw was clenched. He thrust a crumpled note at his sister.

Trixie took the note and stared at it. LEAVE THE MISER ALONE it read.

"That was stuck in the window of the car," Brian said.

"Then there is a miser!" Trixie exclaimed almost joyfully.

Trixie's excitement angered her brother even more. "There's also a vandal," he reminded her. "Someone did who knows how much damage to a valuable antique—one that was entrusted to us. I think that's the important thing right now."

"Of course," Trixie said. "But—"

"But nothing. I'm going to call the police," Brian said. He turned on his heel and walked back into the house.

Trixie followed, her excitement fading as she realized that what Brian had said was true. The damage done to the car wasn't just a possible clue to the mystery of the miser. It was a potential tragedy to the Bob-Whites, who had been trusted with the car because Mr. Burnside thought they were capable of taking care of it until the sale. "Mr. Burnside probably won't let us have the car for the sale now,"

Trixie muttered as she walked to her room. "He probably won't let us use his warehouse for donations." She froze on the top step as the final, most horrible thought occurred to her. "He'll probably even make us pay for the damage! Where will we ever get the money?"

By the time Trixie had changed clothes and come back downstairs, she was on the verge of tears. The noise that had awakened her had been replaced by a pall of silence. Brian and Mart sat tensely at the dining room table.

Trixie slipped noiselessly into a chair across from her brothers.

"Sergeant Molinson is on his way over," Brian told her.

Trixie nodded her head to let her brother know she'd heard him, but she said nothing.

The sound of the sergeant's car coming up the drive finally broke the stillness, and the three Bob-Whites went out to the driveway to meet him.

The sergeant was already inspecting the damage to the Model A. "Not as bad as it might have been," he said.

"Bad enough," Brian answered glumly.

"Can you check the car for fingerprints?" Trixie said. "There must be some way of finding out who did this."

"Oh, I think I already know who did it," Sergeant

Molinson said, stepping back from the car.

The three Beldens stared at him in disbelief. "You do?" Trixie asked.

"It was your hit-and-run victim," the sergeant said. Then he snorted contemptuously.

Trixie stared at Sergeant Molinson as if he'd taken leave of his senses. "But he's in the hospital!" she said.

"Not anymore, he's not," the sergeant told her. "He sneaked out during the night. Nobody noticed he was gone until I went over early this morning to arrest him."

"Arrest him?" Trixie exclaimed. She looked from the sergeant to Brian to Mart, too confused even to ask questions.

"Could you tell us what's going on?" Brian asked. "Let's go inside."

Once again the three Beldens gathered around the dining room table. Sergeant Molinson began to speak as he sat down. "The FBI report came in first thing this morning. The victim's name is Henry Meiser. He escaped last week from a state prison. He was serving a six-month sentence for assault with a deadly weapon." The sergeant stopped to let his words sink in.

Trixie stared at him and asked, "His name is *Miser?* When he was hit by the van, was he talking about finding *himself?*"

"I can't answer that," Sergeant Molinson said after a thoughtful pause. "His name is spelled M-E-I-S-E-R, and he may have meant anything, I guess. It seems that Meiser is the classic eccentric inventor. He's always working on some weird contraption or other. He was harmless enough, though, until a few years ago. Then he claimed he'd had an invention stolen from him. After that, he got more and more secretive. He didn't trust anyone except his secretary, a young widow who had worked for him for a number of years. He wouldn't even patent his inventions, because he was sure that the patent officers were idea thieves."

"That explains it!" Trixie exclaimed.

"Explains what?" Molinson asked sharply.

"When I visited him in the hospital yesterday, he told me about the Stanley brothers—the inventors of the Stanley Steamer. He told how they'd lost control of the rights to their cars. I thought at the time that it sounded as though he was talking about himself. And he was—sort of, at least."

"But what about the assault?" Brian asked.

"Meiser finally went off his rocker completely, I guess," Sergeant Molinson replied. "As I said before, the only person he'd trust was his secretary. He had a janitor, too, who cleaned up the workroom and helped him move heavy things around. One night the janitor was mopping up the floor, when Meiser suddenly flew into a rage. He pulled a gun on the man and accused him of trying to steal his most recent invention."

"What was the invention?" Trixie asked.

The sergeant shrugged. "Nobody knows. Certainly not the janitor. Meiser kept everything in his head and didn't talk to anyone. The janitor testified in court that he didn't know what Meiser was working on, and he didn't care. He just mopped the floors and cashed his paycheck every week."

"Did Mr. Meiser shoot the janitor?" Trixie asked.

"No. As I said, he threatened to. The janitor testified that he threw down his mop and raised his hands. He turned to leave, and Meiser struck him from behind with the butt of his gun. When the janitor came to, he was lying in the alley behind the workshop. The lights in the shop were off, and the door was locked," Sergeant Molinson concluded.

"You keep talking about the janitor's testimony in court," Trixie pointed out. "Did Mr. Meiser admit that it happened the way the janitor said it did?"

"Of course not," the sergeant said. "Meiser stuck to his original story, that the janitor was stealing his invention. He even claimed that the janitor pulled the gun on *him* and that he managed to knock the man on the head with a piece of lead pipe, take the gun away, and haul the man to the alley."

"Couldn't he have been telling the truth, and not

the janitor?" Trixie asked the Sleepyside officer.

"Sure. He *could* have been. Half a dozen witnesses could have been lying, too, when they testified that Meiser had been getting more and more eccentric, convinced that everyone in the world was out to get him. But I don't think that's how it happened," Sergeant Molinson said.

Trixie sat silent for a moment. She remembered her conversation with Henry Meiser. He had seemed eccentric, she had to admit. She herself had used the word "hostile" to describe him. But he certainly hadn't seemed capable of violence. She pictured him in his hospital bed, his head swathed in bandages.

"Wait a minute!" Trixie exclaimed aloud. "We saw him get hit by that van. Was that faked somehow?"

Sergeant Molinson shook his head. "He was hurt, all right. He had a concussion and two cracked ribs. Every step he takes is going to be very painful."

"Then why would he leave the hospital?" Trixie asked.

"I guess he figured a few days in pain beats a few years in prison," the sergeant said. "That's what he'll get if he's caught. He'd have been freed in a couple of months if he hadn't decided to escape." The sergeant shook his head. "I just wish that FBI report had come in a few hours earlier."

Trixie gasped as she suddenly realized why Henry

Meiser had sneaked out of the hospital. *She* had told him about the fingerprint check! As all eyes turned to her, she blushed and stammered, "I—I guess I helped him to escape." Hurrying to explain before he could yell at her, she told the sergeant what she had said to Henry Meiser. She added, "You said he probably wasn't a criminal. I just wanted to make him feel better about having amnesia. Does this make me an accessory to the escape?"

The Glenwood Avenue Connection • 9

SERGEANT MOLINSON SHOOK HIS HEAD RUEFULLY. "I wish I *could* charge you with something. I'd like a judge to sentence you to a year's silence. But I didn't tell you to keep the fingerprinting secret. So it's my responsibility, not yours."

The relief that showed on Trixie's face was quickly replaced by a puzzled look. "Sergeant," she asked, "if Mr. Meiser really was in pain, as you say, why wouldn't he want to get as far away from Sleepyside as possible and just hide a few days until he felt better? Why would he take the time to come clear out here and vandalize the Model A?"

"You young people were the last ones who talked

to Meiser before the accident. After the accident, he couldn't remember what he'd said to you, although that doesn't mean he had total amnesia," Molinson added, flashing a dark look at Trixie. "Obviously, he was afraid he'd said something he shouldn't have. That vandalism was a warning to you that you'd better not tell what you know."

"But what is it that we know?" Trixie demanded.

"I was thinking back over your report of the hit and run while I was driving over here," the sergeant told her. "It seems to me that Glenwood Avenue is the key. We know that's where he was going. We also know he never got there. I think he didn't want anyone else getting there first. I have all the public buildings along Glenwood staked out. I also made sure the officers who patrol Glenwood have Meiser's description. I think that if Meiser does turn up in Sleepyside, that's where he'll be."

"I know—" Trixie broke off as she remembered the haunted eyes of the woman who lived on Glenwood Avenue. She remembered, too, what Honey had said: They had no real proof that the woman was connected with the hit-and-run victim. But a visit from the police would surely terrify her. She might, as Honey suggested, pack up and flee again from whatever unknown danger was frightening her. "I know you'll be able to find him," she concluded awkwardly.

Sergeant Molinson left, and Trixie and her brothers remained seated at the table.

"What do we do now?" Trixie asked.

"Honey and Jim should know about this," Brian said. "Dan and Di, too. I think an emergency meeting of the Bob-Whites is in order."

Trixie nodded, rose from the table and walked to the telephone. She returned a few minutes later and reported, "Honey and Jim and Dan are on their way to the clubhouse now. Di wasn't home. I guess we'll have to fill her in later."

The three Beldens told their mother where they were going and set off for the clubhouse. The Bob-Whites' clubhouse was actually the old gatehouse for the Wheeler estate. The seven club members had shared many happy times there. But, Trixie reflected, looking at her two brothers, who walked with their heads down and their hands jammed in their pockets, this morning's meeting would not be a happy one.

Honey and Jim were waiting at the clubhouse when Trixie and her brothers arrived. Dan hurried in a minute later.

Although Trixie and Jim were copresidents of the club, it was Brian Belden who took charge of this meeting. "What did Trixie tell you on the phone?" he asked.

"Nothing," Honey said, her hazel eyes wide. "She

just asked us to come here right away. Oh, Brian, what's the matter?"

Briefly, Brian told the other three Bob-Whites about the damage to the Model A and their conversation with Sergeant Molinson.

When he told them the sergeant's theory that Glenwood Avenue was a key piece of the puzzle, Honey turned an inquiring gaze on her best friend. Trixie moved her head slightly from left to right, signaling Honey to remain silent. Then she looked down at the table as she realized that Jim had noticed the silent communication between the two girls.

"At any rate," Brian continued, "Mr. Meiser isn't our problem. The Model A is. I wanted to have this meeting so that we could decide, together, what to do about the damage."

"We sure don't have enough money in the treasury to get the car fixed," Dan Mangan grumbled.

"The pecuniary paucity of the treasury is surely legend by now," Mart agreed glumly.

"There's never enough money in the treasury for anything," Trixie said. "I don't understand how it happens, because we all contribute every cent we earn. I put in the money I get for baby-sitting with Bobby, and Honey puts in the money she gets for Moms's mending, and—"

"We all know where the money comes from," Brian said impatiently. "We all know where it goes, too. We had about forty dollars built up in the treasury before we decided to have the rummage sale. Then we bought posters and had fliers printed up and put a couple of ads in the *Sun*. I think we have about fifteen dollars left. But forty or fifteen, it wouldn't begin to cover the cost of four new tires and two new headlights."

"How much will they cost?" Jim asked.

Brian shook his head. "That's the biggest problem we have," he said. "I don't know how much replacement parts are for an antique car. I don't know where to find them, either."

"We're going to have to tell Mr. Burnside what happened," Jim said.

"Oh, woe!" Trixie said. "Do we have to?"

"The Model A is our responsibility, but until it's sold, it's still his car. We have to face the consequences," Jim said firmly.

"But there are so many consequences," Trixie said. "He could take back the car. He could refuse to let us use his lumberyard to store the donations. He could even call off the whole antique car show. And then almost everyone who comes to the sale will be disappointed."

"I think you're getting carried away," Jim said. "He could do all of those things, but I don't think he will. At most, he might take the car back. I couldn't blame him for that."

"Neither could I," Brian agreed. "But I think the best way to keep the other things from happening is to have a plan in mind for paying for the damages when we tell him about them. Could we get back to that subject, please?"

"Couldn't we borrow the money from our parents, just this once?" Honey pleaded.

Jim shook his head. "You know that goes against what this club stands for, Honey. We decided right at the beginning that this was our club and we'd take care of ourselves."

Trixie wrinkled her nose. "Sometimes I wish you weren't so honorable, Jim Frayne," she said.

"I don't think you really mean that," Jim said mildly.

Trixie sighed. "You're right. I don't. I think it's wonderful that you've set aside the whole fortune you inherited from your uncle to establish a school for homeless boys once you've finished college. I think it's wonderful that you're teaching Honey to rely on her own abilities instead of her father's money. I even think it's wonderful that the prize for getting the most donations for the rummage sale is slave labor instead of part of the proceeds. But—"

"Eureka!" Mart Belden shouted. "The ordinarily invalid intellect of my simpering sibling has invented, albeit inadvertently, a delightful denouement to this dilemma."

"Did I say something right for a change?" Trixie asked, blinking owlishly.

Brian nodded, grinning. "I think I know what Mart means," he said. "And it is a wonderful idea."

"It sure is," Dan Mangan agreed.

"I think it is, too, since I thought of it," Trixie said. "But would somebody please tell me what it *is?*"

"When we tell Mr. Burnside about the damage to the car, we'll tell him, at the same time, that we're willing to work off the cost of the repairs," Brian explained with a happy smile.

"Oh," Trixie said. She beamed at the other Bob-Whites. "That *is* a good idea. I'm glad I thought of it."

Brian shoved her teasingly. "The brains of the Belden family," he jested.

Trixie continued to smile, and her friends smiled back. It was a relief to have the problem solved.

"There's something else to think about," Jim said, his smile fading. "The damage to the car wasn't accidental, remember? It was vandalism. Do we dare to keep that car until the sale? Do we even dare to put it on display, along with a lot of others that might be more valuable, and risk having them ruined, too?"

"I really don't see that as a problem," Brian said. "The vandal was Henry Meiser. He made his point.

He's probably long gone by now. He won't risk coming back, especially when there's a crowd around."

"I think you're right about the cars being safe," Trixie said. "But I'm not sure I believe that Mr. Meiser was the vandal."

"Sergeant Molinson believes it. I think I'm willing to take his word for it, unless you can think of a better suspect," Brian told her.

"I bet I can give you three good reasons for Mr. Meiser *not* being the best suspect," Trixie retorted.

"I'm listening," Brian told her, folding his arms across his chest.

"Well," Trixie said slowly, trying to organize her thoughts, "first of all, there's the note that was left on the car. 'Leave the miser alone.' If Mr. Meiser wrote that note, why wouldn't he spell his name right?"

"Perchance it was an attempt at subtlety," Mart said, "a clever alteration of his own cognomen."

"Or there might be a small-*m* miser that Henry capital-*m* Meiser is looking for," Brian said. "That was our first thought, the night of the accident. Maybe there's a miser on Glenwood Avenue, after all."

"But none of us remembers hearing about a miser in all of Sleepyside," Trixie told her brother.

"It might not be a miser we'd have heard about," Dan said. "What I mean is, Sergeant Molinson told you Mr. Meiser had accused someone of stealing an invention from him. Maybe he just started calling the thief a miser, because the thief was keeping the profits of the invention to himself, instead of sharing them."

"But how could he have expected us to know what his nickname was for the thief? How could he have expected us to know there was a thief?" Trixie asked.

"He doesn't remember what he said right before the accident, remember?" Brian said.

"I remember that he doesn't remember. I was there when he told me he didn't remember. Remember?" Trixie returned her brother's teasing of the day before. "Anyway, I don't have to have a solution for what 'the miser' is. All I have to do is point out that it doesn't make sense for Mr. Meiser to have written that on the note, if he was the vandal."

"All right," Brian said wearily. "I'll give you one point for that one. What are the other two?"

Trixie snapped her fingers as another thought occurred to her. "Henry Meiser told us cars were his passion. I could tell they were from the way he talked about them in the hospital. If he wanted to do something to scare us, the last thing he'd do would be to vandalize an antique car."

"I can turn that argument right around to prove it *was* Henry Meiser who vandalized the car," Brian said. "Someone who didn't love cars wouldn't have stopped with slashed tires and broken headlights if they wanted to vandalize a car. They seem like big items to us, but those are probably the two most easily replaced items on the Model A. Mr. Meiser would have picked the car to vandalize because he'd know we'd associate him with it. But he'd pull his punches for the car's sake, not ours."

"What's your third point?" Dan asked.

"The man I talked to in the hospital yesterday just wasn't the type to do anything destructive," Trixie said stubbornly.

"He went to prison for committing assault," Brian said. "That's pretty destructive."

"End of round three," Jim said softly. "I'm afraid you haven't convinced any of us, Trix."

"Well, I've convinced myself, anyway," Trixie told him. "And I'm more sure than ever about something else."

"What's that?" Jim asked.

"Henry Meiser's hit-and-run accident was no accident. Somebody ran him down intentionally."

"Not that theory again!" Brian exclaimed.

"Well, think about it. If Mr. Meiser *wasn't* the one who vandalized the car, somebody else *was*. But it must be somebody connected with him, because he was connected with the car," Trixie said.

"And that just logically leads you to the conclusion that somebody ran him down on purpose,"

Brian said, shaking his head. "I wish they offered a course in logic at Sleepyside Junior-Senior High School. I'd force you to sign up for it."

"No," Mart said. "Such overt cruelty would be unwarranted. Our distaff sibling would be incapable of attaining a passing grade in such a course. She would become the oldest freshman enrolled in our alma mater."

Trixie flushed and opened her mouth to speak, but Brian gestured for silence. "I'm sorry about my wisecrack, Trixie. I really am. It may turn out that your hunch is right and someone did run Mr. Meiser down intentionally. But there's nothing we can do about that now. We *can* call Mr. Burnside and tell him about the car. I think we'd better go do that."

"Meeting adjourned," Jim said, rising from his chair. "Let's go over to Manor House to make the call. That's the closest phone. I don't mind admitting I'd like to have this over with."

The four boys rose and walked to the door. Trixie remained seated, resting her chin on her hand. Honey continued to sit across the table, looking at her best friend anxiously.

"Are you girls coming along?" Jim asked over his shoulder.

Honey shook her head and motioned for her brother to go on ahead. Jim nodded understandingly.

"They were pretty hard on you, Trixie," Honey

said softly when the door had closed behind the boys.

"That's what I get for telling them my theories. Sergeant Molinson said today that he'd like to sentence me to a year's silence. I wish he would!" Trixie said hotly.

"Well, you convinced me, anyway," Honey said. "I don't think Mr. Meiser was the vandal, either."

"You're not just saying that, are you?" Trixie asked.

Honey shook her head. "At least you convinced me that the case isn't as cut-and-dried as Sergeant Molinson made it sound. If the boys knew about the woman on Glenwood Avenue—"

"They'd tell me she was afraid of Henry Meiser or of something totally unrelated," Trixie concluded. "I thought about telling them, but I knew Brian and Mart would have a fit because I didn't say anything when Sergeant Molinson was at the house today."

"That's right!" Honey said. "Oh, Trixie, you should have told *him*!"

"Probably," Trixie admitted. "I was about to, but I remembered what you said. I don't want to make that woman more terrified than she already is."

"Trixie Belden, when I said that, Henry Meiser hadn't left Sleepyside Hospital in the middle of the night!" Honey said. "Even if he didn't vandalize the Model A, everything is different now."

"Nothing is different," Trixie protested. "We still

have no good reason to believe that woman is connected with Henry Meiser."

"We don't have any good reasons, but you do believe it, don't you?" Honey guessed.

Trixie grinned sheepishly. "You're reading my thoughts again, Honey. I do think there's a connection. That's why I want to go back to that house, right now!"

"Go back!" Honey exclaimed. "Oh, Trixie, we can't do that! How will we explain it to the boys?"

"We don't have to. They'll be busy with the car all afternoon. We'll just tell our parents we have an errand to run in town."

"But what can you hope to find out by going back to the house?" Honey asked.

"I don't know," Trixie admitted. "But it's the only way I can think of to get some proof that that woman is connected with Henry Meiser. Once we have proof, we'll go to the police. I promise."

Honey sighed. "There's no point in arguing. Your mind is made up. Let's go."

Half an hour later, the two girls were biking slowly along Glenwood Avenue, trying to look as though they were out for a leisurely ride. Only Trixie's glowing face showed how fast they had pedaled to get there.

"Look," Trixie whispered. "There are two kids

playing hopscotch in front of the house. And one of them is the little girl we saw the other day."

Trixie stopped her bike in front of the house, holding herself upright with a foot against the curb. "Hi!" she called. "It's a nice day for hopscotch."

The little girl paused, wobbling on one foot. She bent to pick up her stone and hopped to the end of the pattern chalked on the walk. "It's nice to be outside," she said, walking over to Trixie and Honey.

"That's right. You weren't supposed to play outside," Trixie prompted.

"That was before," the little girl said. "We always played outside until we moved here. Then we couldn't for a while, and now we can again!"

"I'm glad," Trixie said. "It's no fun to be in the house all the time."

The little girl shook her head solemnly. "It sure isn't. It seemed like months and months before we got to go out."

"Were you sick?" Trixie asked. "Is that why you couldn't go out?"

"I told you I wasn't," the little girl said. "It kind of seemed like Mommy was, though. She cried all the time. Except sometimes she yelled. She doesn't usually yell. She's happier now, though, ever since Uncle Hank came to visit."

Trixie felt a sudden chill as the little girl's words registered on her mind. Uncle Hank was here for a

167

visit—and Hank was a nickname for Henry!

"How long ago did Uncle Hank get here?" Trixie asked, trying to sound casual.

"Oh, just—" The little girl's reply was interrupted by her mother.

"Melissa, you get in here this minute! Can't I trust you at all? Come on! Davey, you, too!" the woman shrieked.

"Oh-oh. Mommy's mad again. I gotta go." The little girl turned and ran back toward the house, pushing her little brother ahead of her.

Trixie and Honey stared at the two children as they ran into the house. "Well," Trixie said, "there's our connection."

Held Hostage! • 10

HONEY WAS THE FIRST to rouse herself and start pedaling slowly down Glenwood Avenue once more. Trixie remained, staring at the house for a moment. Then she began to follow her friend.

"I guess it's time to go to Sergeant Molinson, isn't it?" Honey asked softly. She waited for Trixie's reply, and when none came, she repeated more loudly, "Isn't it?"

"I don't know," Trixie said slowly.

"Trixie!" Honey's voice was raised in exasperation. "You said before that we couldn't tell the sergeant about the woman in the house because there was no real proof of a connection between her and Henry Meiser. 'Uncle Hank' is the proof of a connection. What possible reason can you have for wanting to wait any longer?"

"The reason I want to wait longer is that I think I've waited too long already," Trixie said.

"That makes no sense at all," Honey told her.

"You'd think it makes sense if you'd seen Sergeant Molinson's face turning as purple as a plum this morning when he found out I'd told Mr. Meiser about the fingerprint check," Trixie said miserably.

"It seems to me that's all the more reason for going to him right now and telling him about this house," Honey said. "He'll stop being angry as soon as he has Henry Meiser back in custody."

"And he'll start being angry again when he finds out we've known that there was something strange going on in that house for the past few days and didn't say anything," Trixie retorted.

Honey thought about that for a moment. "You're right. He'll tell us we should have let him do the deciding about what's suspicious and what isn't, instead of taking it on ourselves," she said finally.

"He said this morning that he wished he could charge me with something," Trixie said. "When he finds out about this, he'll probably start leafing through the law books for something that carries a life sentence."

Honey giggled at her friend's exaggerated gloom.

"I really don't think it will be that bad, Trix. It won't be any fun to face him, though. But I don't see what else we can do."

"We could just wait a day or two and see if the police catch Mr. Meiser," Trixie said hopefully. "Sergeant Molinson knows he's here on Glenwood Avenue. It's probably only a matter of time until they find the house."

Honey shook her head. "I don't think that would be the right thing to do," she said. "First of all, we know that Mr. Meiser is hurt. I think he'd be better off back in custody, where he'd at least be in the prison ward of a hospital.

"And second, what about that woman and her children? I'd hate to see them hurt, and they could be if the police stumble onto the house and Henry Meiser gets desperate."

"Oh, woe!" Trixie said. "You're right both times, Honey."

"Then we'll go to the police," Honey said firmly. She turned her bike in a wide arc and started back toward the downtown section of Sleepyside.

Trixie turned slowly to follow. She coasted for a moment, then she pedaled quickly to catch up with Honey. "I have an idea!" she said hoarsely.

"Oh, no," Honey groaned.

"Now wait—just listen to what I have to say," Trixie pleaded. "Suppose Henry Meiser decides to

171

turn himself in. If he goes to the police station by himself, the woman and her children won't be in any trouble. And nobody will ever have to know that we knew he was in that house."

"That's a wonderful idea, all right," Honey said flatly. "As soon as I get home, I'll get out my lucky rabbit's foot, and when it gets dark, I'll make a wish on the first star for Mr. Meiser to turn himself in."

"No," Trixie said scornfully. "I mean we could talk Mr. Meiser into turning himself in."

Honey stopped riding and propped herself against a curb. She stared at Trixie as if her friend had taken leave of her senses.

"It's so simple!" Trixie exclaimed. "We'll come back tonight after dinner. We'll tell the woman who lives there that we know Mr. Meiser is there, but we haven't told the police. That will get her trust. Then we'll ask her if we can talk to him."

"And he'll hit us on the head with something and escape again. How will we explain that to Sergeant Molinson?" Honey asked.

"I don't think he'll hurt us, Honey." She clapped her hands over her ears as she saw Honey start to protest. "I know, I know. He's been convicted of assault, and that proves he's dangerous. But it doesn't—it doesn't prove anything to me, I mean. I talked to Henry Meiser for a long time at the hospital. I just don't think he's a violent person."

"If I tell you I won't come back here tonight, what will you do?" Honey asked.

"I'll come alone," Trixie answered firmly.

"And if I call Sergeant Molinson this afternoon and tell him where to find Henry Meiser, will you ever forgive me?" Honey asked.

Trixie didn't answer.

"All right," Honey sighed. "We'll come back tonight after dinner."

At seven-thirty, the two girls were hurrying down Glenwood Avenue toward the mysterious house, where they were sure Henry Meiser was hiding.

"Do you think Brian and Mart believed you when you said we wanted to canvass for the rummage sale tonight to make up for the work they did on the Model A today?" Honey asked.

"They must have. Brian offered to drive us to Sleepyside and pick us up, didn't he? I think they were just so relieved that Mr. Burnside wasn't angry that they weren't thinking about anything else," Trixie answered.

"It is perfectly perfect of Mr. Burnside to help them find replacement parts and let them keep the car for the sale and everything," Honey said.

"It's 'perfectly perfect' that his insurance policy on the car only had a fifty dollar deduction, or whatever you call it," Trixie added. "We'll be able to work that off in one afternoon." She paused to catch her breath. The mysterious house was only half a block away. "I just wish Brian had given us more time."

"We have all the time we need," Honey said. "If we can't persuade Henry Meiser to give himself up in the next hour, we'll never be able to."

The girls paused in front of the house.

"Well, here goes," Trixie said. She moved slowly up the walk. She stopped and started to turn as she heard Honey's stifled scream.

Then a hand was clapped over Trixie's mouth, and a harsh voice said, "Just one noise from you girls, and it's the last one you'll ever make!"

Trixie gritted her teeth to keep the scream that was rising in her throat from escaping. She felt herself being half-dragged across the lawn. Above the hand that was still clamped tightly across her nose and mouth, Trixie saw a vehicle parked at the curb. She knew that their captor was pushing them toward the open back doors of a green van!

Trixie and Honey landed hard on the floor of the van, and the doors slammed behind them while they were still pulling themselves upright.

Trixie drew in deep breaths, grateful that at least the suffocating hand had been removed. She felt Honey's icy hand clench her arm, and she covered her friend's hand with her own.

Their captor hoisted himself into the driver's seat and put the van in gear.

"I know who you are," Trixie said. "You're the man who ran down Henry Meiser!"

The driver chuckled. "That's not who I am at all, young lady. That's what I *did*. Who I am is Andy Kowalski." He turned and looked at the girls with a nasty smile on his face. "I knocked old Hank down the other night, all right. But I was just returning a favor, so to speak," the man continued.

The statement clicked in Trixie's churning mind. "You're the man who used to work for Mr. Meiser— the one he assaulted."

"He told you about that, did he?" Andy Kowalski guessed. "I knew you kids were chummy with the old coot, but I didn't know you were that close."

"He didn't tell us anything," Honey protested.

"Sure. You just figured it out for yourselves," Andy Kowalski said sarcastically.

"I can see why you'd want to get revenge on Henry Meiser, after what he did to you," Trixie said in what she hoped was a soothing voice. "But how do we fit into that?"

Andy Kowalski chuckled. "It isn't revenge I'm after, young lady," he said. "Revenge and forty cents will get you a pack of gum these days. No, I'm after money in the bank. I'm going to use you girls to get hold of the miser."

"The miser again!" Trixie exclaimed. "Who *is* the miser?"

"Are you kidding?" he asked, sounding genuinely surprised. "No, I guess you probably aren't. Old Hank would have to get pretty close to somebody to tell them he'd come up with the most revolutionary new invention in a hundred years."

Honey and Trixie exchanged astonished glances.

The man chuckled again. "Well, I guess the joke's on me. That little note I left for you kids must not have meant a thing to you. I'm glad I didn't pay for a stamp!"

"Then you're the one who vandalized the Model A!" Trixie said.

"Who'd you think it was, Santa Claus?" he growled. "I saw you kids with Meiser the night I ran him down. I saw you going to visit Eileen, his secretary. I saw you coming out of his room at the hospital. So I knew you must have got friendly with the old weirdo somehow. He was always real good to Eileen's kids, buying them toys at Christmas and all. I figured maybe young people in general were the only ones he trusted. I also figured he might trust you to get the miser hidden away somewhere, once he knew I'd tracked him to Sleepyside and most of the way to Eileen's hideout."

Andy Kowalski pulled the van over to the curb. He reached into the front of his shirt and pulled out a gun. "I'll be back in a minute. And I won't go so far that a few of these bullets couldn't catch up with you if you try to run away," he said, gesturing with the gun. "So you just wait right here." He climbed out of the van, laughing at the joke he'd just made.

Trixie leaned over the front seat and looked out the side window of the van. "He's going into a telephone booth," she reported. "Who could he possibly be calling?"

"Who cares?" Honey whimpered. "The question is, how are we going to get out of here? I don't like that man."

Trixie shivered and rubbed her arms hard to quell the goosebumps that had risen on them. "I don't like him, either," she said. "I hate the way he keeps making dumb little jokes and laughing at them. It's as if he doesn't even know he's doing anything wrong."

"I know," Honey said. "Imagine calling that hit and run the return of a favor! I think he's really dangerous, Trixie!"

Trixie patted Honey's shoulder clumsily. "We'll get out of this someway, Honey. Don't worry."

Andy Kowalski returned to the van, started it up again, and then turned back toward the house where Henry Meiser was hiding. He didn't speak, but he hummed a tune to himself, keeping time by tapping his fingers on the steering wheel.

He pulled over to the curb directly across the

street from the house. He put the car in park but left the motor running. "Ready when you are, Hank," he muttered.

"Is Henry Meiser coming out here?" Trixie asked.

"He will if he knows what's good for *you*," their captor said. "You young ladies should feel honored. Hank must value you pretty highly if he's willing to trade you for the miser."

"This isn't the first time you've tried to take the miser from him, is it?" Trixie asked.

Andy Kowalski sneered. "He *did* tell you that whole story, then. Well, *you* can believe what you like. I got the *jury* to believe me! Yes, sir, it's too bad they don't give out awards to thieves. I'd get first prize, that's for sure. You should have seen me when I was working for old Hank. I acted like I didn't have sense enough to pound sand in a rathole. I'd just sweep up around the place, pretending like I didn't even hear old Hank muttering to himself while he worked on the miser. I'd pick things up and dust under them and put them down like I hadn't even seen what they were. But I was watching and listening, all right.

"I waited till the day Meiser said, 'Now, my little friend, you're ready for testing.' He did that—talked to the hunk of metal that he'd invented like it was a real person.

"Anyway, I knew then I could make off with it

and get it patented and keep the profits for myself. Hank was such a perfectionist that he wouldn't have said something was ready for testing unless it was danged near perfect. He was such a distrustful old coot that he wouldn't have it patented, either, until he'd already gotten money for the rights.

"Anyway, I sneaked into the shop that night. Hank had fallen asleep in a chair in the back room. He heard me moving around and came out screaming. I pulled my gun on him, but he didn't even seem to notice it. He just wanted to keep me from stealing the miser. He picked up a piece of lead pipe and threw it at me so fast I didn't have time to duck.

"Then he made his big mistake. He wouldn't call the cops, because he was afraid someone would find out about his invention. He just hauled me out into the alley and tossed my gun out after me. That left his prints on the gun, of course, and that really clinched my story for the jury," Andy Kowalski gloated.

"Then Mr. Meiser was telling the truth in court," Trixie said, feeling relieved that her feelings about him had been confirmed.

"Mostly he was. But he lied about the most important thing of all—what he was working on. You see, even when he thought he might go to jail, the only thing he cared about was the miser. He had Eileen hide it away for him, and he brought some worthless

179

scrap of tin that he said was a new electronic thing-amajig. My lawyer made a big thing about how that wasn't worth stealing, so the jury didn't see why I'd have broken into the shop to steal it."

Trixie shook her head. Henry Meiser's distrust of people was what had really gotten him into trouble, after all.

"Meiser got six months in jail," Kowalski continued. "I figured that would be long enough for me to get hold of the miser. But I hadn't reckoned on Eileen dropping completely out of sight. I always thought she was in love with Meiser, but I didn't think she was so crazy about him that she'd give up her house and pack up her kids and move away. That's just what she did, though. I couldn't find a trace of her."

"How *did* you finally find her?" Trixie asked.

Andy Kowalski didn't answer immediately. He peered out the window of the van at the house, which still showed no sign of activity. He held his watch close to his eyes to see how much time had elapsed since his phone call to Henry Meiser.

"I didn't find her. Meiser did," he said finally. "I figured that was the only way. I bribed a friend of mine who was in jail with Meiser to organize an escape. Then I just followed Hank to Sleepyside. He was cagey about it and didn't go right to Eileen's house. He checked into a cheap hotel first."

Kowalski chortled. "He should have tried a fancier one—where all the outgoing calls from the rooms didn't go through the hotel switchboard—or at least one where the operator wasn't so easy to bribe. She gave me the number Meiser called, found out the street address for that number, and repeated the whole conversation the minute he hung up.

"I could have gone right to Eileen's house, but I decided to follow Hank, just to see what kind of tricks he might pull. I saw him stop to talk to you young people. And while I waited, I realized I didn't need Hank anymore. I knew where the miser was, and I didn't care whether the cops or the coroner got him first."

Trixie shuddered. Honey had been right—Andy Kowalski had no sense of right or wrong. He was like a child who only cared about getting his own way, with no thought about what pain he might cause getting it. She felt as though she'd heard all she wanted to.

"I kept underestimating Eileen, though," their captor continued. "When Hank didn't show up on schedule, she locked that house up as tight as a drum. I couldn't get to her or her kids without breaking the door down, and that would have brought the cops down on my neck. I went from this house to the hospital and back again, waiting for something to break. Wouldn't you know, I'd taken an hour off to get some sleep, when Hank left the hospital and came here. I almost had a chance to snatch the kids this afternoon, but then you two came along and scared them off."

Their captor checked his watch again. "I guess I owe you girls something for that, don't I? And I just might pay off, if Meiser doesn't show his face pretty soon."

As if on cue, a crack of light appeared at the front door of the house across the street. The crack widened, and Henry Meiser stepped outside.

The Drop · 11

TRIXIE RECOGNIZED Henry Meiser immediately, although the white bandages were no longer on his head. He walked stiffly, one arm held to his stomach as though his ribs were still giving him a lot of pain. From the other hand dangled a large brown paper bag. It banged against his leg with every other step he took.

Trixie expected to see him come to the van, but instead he started off down the sidewalk on the other side of the street.

"That's it," Andy Kowalski said, putting the car in gear. "At least, that better be it, or you girls are in big trouble."

"What's happening, Trixie?" Honey whispered into her friend's ear.

Trixie shook her head. The same question was running through her own mind, but she had no idea how to answer it.

She thought frantically, trying to piece together the information she had. "That better be it," their captor had said. He must have been referring to the miser, since that was what he had come to the house to get. That meant the miser was—or should be—in the paper bag.

The plan must be for the inventor to drop the bag off somewhere. Once Andy Kowalski was sure that the miser was really there, he'd let the girls go—she hoped.

"That better be it." The phrase repeated itself in Trixie's mind. But *was* that it? Henry Meiser had been willing to go to prison rather than to reveal what the miser was. Would he give it up to save two girls he hardly knew?

Trixie remembered what Mr. Meiser had said the night of the hit and run and again that day at the hospital. "Don't get involved" was Henry Meiser's motto. "Don't trust anyone" was the primary rule by which he lived his life.

"We're involved with you now, Mr. Meiser." Her lips moved, but no sound came out. "Oh, please, please don't let us down. We're more important than any invention." She could only hope that Henry Meiser was thinking the same thing.

She wondered suddenly who had thought of the drop-off. That would make a big difference. If it had been the inventor's idea, it could mean that he hoped to drop off another worthless scrap of tin and get away, leaving the girls captive. Meanwhile, Eileen could take her children—and the real miser—and run away again.

Or would Mr. Meiser even care if he got away, as long as his invention was safe? Andy Kowalski had said he talked to the invention as if it were a real person. Would he be willing to protect it with his life, as parents sometimes did for their children?

Trixie held her breath as the driver pulled the van over to the curb. But nothing happened. He just sat, car still in gear, for a few moments.

"Meiser's moving like a turtle," he muttered. "His ribs must be giving him fits. He's making a sitting duck out of me, creeping down the road after him. But I can't let him get too far ahead, in case he decides to make a break for it."

The van idled for a few more moments, until Meiser was a block down the street, then glided down the street once more.

The stop-and-go pattern continued. The injured man walked stiffly, his arm still curved protectively around his ribs. He didn't stop or look back or even glance around him. "That's a good boy," Andy Kowalski murmured. "You keep right on going like I told you to."

Trixie's stomach flip-flopped at the driver's words. *He'd* told him to go this way. That must mean the whole plan had been his.

"Maybe not," she whispered to herself. "It might have been a compromise he worked out when Mr. Meiser refused to come to the van."

"What did you say, Trixie?" Honey whispered, moving closer in the dim light in the back of the van.

"I need to know whose idea it was for Mr. Meiser to get away from the house to drop off the bag," Trixie whispered.

"But why—" Honey broke off as she realized why that information was important. "You don't think Mr. Meiser would try to trick Andy Kowalski, do you?"

"Of course not," Trixie said hastily, trying to keep Honey from getting more upset. "Not really," she added less certainly.

"Where are we going?" Honey blurted to their captor.

Trixie felt a lump in her throat. She had tried to keep herself from knowing. Now she was going to know, once and for all.

"We're going where Meiser goes," the driver said tauntingly. He pulled the van to the side of the street once again. He turned around and glanced at the girls. "But that doesn't answer your question, does it? Well, we're going to a couple of places. We're going to a trash can at the edge of Memorial Park first. After we leave there, we're going to the Sleepyside police station."

"To the police?" Trixie exclaimed.

Andy Kowalski laughed his maddening laugh. "Does that surprise you? Well, I've got nothing against police stations. Some of them are really pretty, too, especially in little towns like this. Yessir, I kind of like to look at them—from the outside!" He snorted as he pulled out into the street again, then stepped on the brakes and muttered something under his breath as Meiser stopped suddenly, leaning against a fence in somebody's front yard and bending over at the waist.

"Why doesn't the fool just put up a billboard, if he's so anxious to attract attention?" Kowalski said.

"He's hurt!" Trixie said defensively.

"He's going to hurt a lot worse if he doesn't keep going. And so will you, if you don't keep quiet!" The van lurched a little—as if punctuating their captor's angry threat—when it finally started down the street once more.

Trixie bit her lips and sagged against the wall of the van. Memorial Park was still blocks away. It must be almost a mile to the park from where they'd started out. That was a long, painful walk for a man with broken ribs and a concussion. What if he didn't make it? Or what if his labored walking did attract someone's attention? Would Andy Kowalski give up his plan and let the girls go? Trixie stared at the back of their captor's head. Somehow, she didn't think so.

"Mr. Kowalski," Honey said softly, "would you please tell us where we're going?"

"I did tell you!" he shouted. The strain of waiting for Meiser was beginning to show on him. Even his twisted sense of humor was deserting him. "I told you what I came to Sleepyside for, and that's what I'm going to get. Before too long, I'll have the miser, and old Hank will be safely in the arms of the police."

The pieces finally fit together in Trixie's mind. "Your plan is for Mr. Meiser to drop the invention off in the trash can at the park, then go to the police station and turn himself in. That's what you told him he had to do before you'd let us go!"

"Of course," their captor said, as if it had been obvious all along. "You don't think I want to get close to Meiser again, do you? Not after what happened back at the workshop!" He shook his head. "I just don't trust him not to pull something funny. He defends that invention like a she-bear protects her cub.

"When he makes the drop, I'll have plenty of time

to check that it really is the miser this time, while he walks on to the police station. And once he's inside, I'll have plenty of time to get away, even if he does manage to convince the police that I robbed him— which he won't!"

Memorial Park was now in sight, but Henry Meiser had sagged against another fence.

"What if he can't make it to the police station?" Trixie asked in concern.

Andy Kowalski shrugged. "If he collapses, somebody'll find him and call the police. It all amounts to the same thing. I'll just have a little more time to get away, that's all."

"Haven't you forgotten about us?" Honey demanded. "As soon as you let us go, we'll call the police."

Andy Kowalski threw back his head and laughed, slapping his thigh to show how much her remark amused him. "That's right; I forgot you girls could talk. You've been so quiet all the while." His laughter ceased abruptly, and he turned to look at the girls. His eyes glittered, as cold as ice. "I guess I'll have to be sure that doesn't happen, won't I?"

Trixie felt frightened, but angry tears welled in her eyes. How stupid she'd been to think Henry Meiser was the one they had to worry about! This evil man had never intended to let them go at all! For a moment, she found herself half-wishing that

Mr. Meiser's precious invention wasn't in the brown paper bag. It would be foolish for him to give it up in vain.

Trixie realized quickly that it was just as foolish to waste time making wishes. She had to do something —but what?

She found herself wondering what time it was. Brian had only given the girls an hour. Surely that much time had elapsed since he'd dropped them off. At first, Trixie knew, he'd wait patiently for them. How long would it take before he became alarmed?

And what good would it do if Brian knew they were missing? He wouldn't know where to start looking for them.

Jim would, though! Trixie's heart leaped at the thought. Jim had known about Trixie's interest in the house on Glenwood Avenue. That would be the very first place he'd go if he knew that the girls had disappeared.

Trixie tried to think through what would happen next. Probably nothing, she realized with a sinking heart. Eileen would not open the door to anyone until she heard from Henry Meiser. If the boys went to the house, they'd conclude that it was empty, then give up and go home.

She and Honey had no hope of help from the outside, Trixie admitted to herself. They would have to help themselves.

Poor Honey! Trixie looked at the huddled figure next to her. "I'm sorry I got you into this mess," she whispered to her best friend.

"Let's just get *out* of it," Honey whispered back. Her tone was neither angry nor frightened. Instead, it was filled with a grim determination. Honey was more timid than Trixie about plunging into mysteries, but she was far from spineless in the face of trouble.

"We'll think of something," Trixie promised.

She looked up as she felt the van slow down again. They were at the edge of Memorial Park, she realized with a jolt.

Henry Meiser was crossing the street directly in front of the van. But the van might have been invisible, for all Meiser seemed to notice. He continued to stare straight ahead.

Trixie bit her lower lip as she saw the inventor's face in the glare of the van's headlights. It was as white as chalk. The man looked twenty years older than he had the night he'd stopped to help the Bob-Whites with their stalled car.

Trixie tried to imagine the torment he was going through. The physical pain from his broken ribs and concussion would be bad enough. But added to it was the emotional burden of giving up his precious invention—or, she forced herself to add, of betraying the two girls who were being held captive by a man whose treachery he knew all too well.

Trixie followed Meiser's tortured journey with her eyes. Goosebumps rose once again on her arms when she saw the trash can that Meiser was walking toward. Honey's gasp told Trixie that her friend, too, had spotted the drop-off point.

Meiser showed no signs of hesitation as he walked to the trash can, shoved the bag inside, turned, and started back down the sidewalk.

Andy Kowalski reached into the front of his shirt and drew out a gun. He turned and pointed it first at Trixie and then at Honey. "I thought I'd be able to trust one of you girls to play retriever for me," he said. "But you got too smart. You've already figured out you'd have nothing to lose by running away. So I'm going to leave you right here. I'll give you one word of advice: *Don't.* Don't try to run. By the time you open a door, I'll be back. I'll have my friend here ready for you, too," he said, gesturing with the gun.

He crawled out of the van and ran toward the trash can.

His final words of warning had given Trixie the idea she had been looking for. She leaned over the front seat and punched down the button on the door lock.

"Quick, Honey!" she said. "Lock the other side. Then hit the deck!"

Honey reacted instantly.

"He could put a bullet through the side of the van," Honey whispered.

"He could," Trixie said aloud, feeling bold now that she had taken some action on her own behalf. "But it wouldn't do him any good. All he'd do would be to bring the police down on himself."

"Hey!" Andy Kowalski had discovered the locked doors. He pounded on them with his fists. "Let me in!"

Stretched out on the cold metal floor of the van, Trixie barely stifled a hysterical giggle. "What was that he said about pounding sand in a rathole?" she said to Honey.

Honey's pent-up breath escaped in a quavering echo of Trixie's giggle. "I had a feeling Mr. Kowalski wasn't as smart as he kept telling us he was," she said.

The girls fell silent as they heard him pounding against the glass with the butt of his gun.

"Oh, Trixie, if he breaks through that glass he'll be able to unlock the door and get inside. What will we do then?" Honey asked, terrified.

Trixie didn't have to answer that question—the sound of police sirens screaming toward them answered it for her.

"Freeze, Kowalski!" the familiar voice of Sergeant Molinson shouted. "You're under arrest!"

Trixie sat up to look through the window. "Honey, there must be five squad cars out there! They're all around us! And Henry Meiser is standing right on the sidewalk, watching everything!"

Meiser's Miser • 12

TRIXIE HAD NO TIME TO REST the next two days. There were statements to give to the police, explanations to make to her worried brothers and parents, hours of door-to-door rounds asking for donations for the rummage sale, a flurry of last-minute phone calls to remind donors to deliver their merchandise, and pricing and arranging the donations in the school gymnasium.

The final piece of merchandise for the sale was tagged and put in place just half an hour before the sale was scheduled to begin. Trixie and Honey sank wearily into chairs at the table next to the gymnasium door, where customers would be paying for the rummage they had selected.

"If we only sell half of what's here in the gym, we'll be at our original goal," Jim said as he walked up to the table. He had taken responsibility for totaling the donations. He looked down at the figures he'd written in the notebook he was carrying and added, "And that doesn't count the Model A *or* the food booth."

"Yippee!" Trixie shouted, her fatigue completely forgotten.

"That's not all," Jim said. "The sale of the Model A has turned into an auction. Three buyers turned up early this morning, all ready to write a check. So Mr. Burnside told them to write down how much they're willing to pay. We'll look at those offers— and at any others we get—this afternoon and sell to whoever has offered the most. We might get a lot more than we'd hoped for."

"That's the good news," Honey said. "Is there any bad news we should know about?"

Jim grinned at his sister, knowing that she was referring to their Bob-Whites' contest, which Mr. Burnside had agreed to judge. "Well, there is bad news, of course. We knew there would be. The question is this: Whom is it bad for?"

"Oh, Jim, don't tease!" Trixie protested. "Who won the contest—and who lost?"

"Well, unless someone demands a recount, it looks

as though Mart and Di are about to become the unwilling slaves of—" Jim paused for effect and looked
at Trixie and Honey—"Dan and me!"

Trixie felt curiously disappointed. "We didn't win
or lose."

"Nope. You came in a close second, and Brian and
the Model A were third," Jim said.

"Just don't be too easy on Mart," Trixie said stern-
ly. "If you need help thinking of things for him to
do, I'll be happy to give you the list I'd worked out in
my mind."

"I'm sure I'll think of a few dirty and disgusting
chores," Jim said with a grin. "I'm going out to the
parking lot right now to break the news."

"We'll come along," Trixie said, jumping up from
her chair. "We've been in here all morning, and
we'll be here most of the afternoon. This is probably
our only chance to see the car show when it isn't
swarming with people."

Out in the parking lot, Mart, Di, Dan, and Brian
were helping Mr. Burnside arrange the cars for
display. The job was more difficult than it sounded,
because the proud owners were there, too, each
demanding that his car get the best possible display
spot.

The owners whose cars were already in place were
going over them with polishing rags, wiping off im-
aginary fingerprints.

"This has turned into a first-class show," Mr. Burnside said, looking over the cars on display. "Just about every really great car you could think of is represented."

"Look at that beautiful car over there," Honey said.

Mr. Burnside nodded his head approvingly. "You have excellent taste. This is a Bugatti, one of the most beautiful and admired of the classic cars."

"Is that the kind of car you want to buy next?" Trixie asked.

Mr. Burnside shook his head regretfully. "Bugattis are the most beautiful and admired, but they're also the most difficult to own and maintain. Bugatti owners simply accept the fact that every time they drive their cars, they'll wind up pulling over to the side of the road to tinker with the plugs or the radiator. That kind of thing isn't for me."

"At least you wouldn't have to do all that tinkering to get the car started, as you do with the Steamer," Trixie pointed out.

"That's what you think," Mr. Burnside said. "If it's at all cold, you have to drain the radiator and put in hot water. You have to empty the oil out of the crankcase, heat it on the stove, and pour it back in. You have to hand-crank the engine, because the electric starter won't work. You have to let the car idle at least ten minutes at high speed, so that the plugs won't get clogged with oil. Then you're ready to go—until the car breaks down somewhere along the road."

"Gleeps!" Trixie exclaimed. "Why didn't they make a better car than that?"

"There is no better car when it's working right," Mr. Burnside told her. "It drives as though it's alive, as though it has a brain that understands exactly where you want it to go. That's what Bugatti was aiming for. He was an artist—he actually studied sculpture. The everyday concerns of the driver were of no interest to him. There's a story that someone once complained to Bugatti about the difficulties in getting one of his cars started on cold mornings. Bugatti sniffed, looked down his nose, and said, 'Keep the car in a heated garage.'"

"Another eccentric inventor," Trixie mused. For the first time that day, she thought about Henry Meiser.

As if reading her thoughts, Brian said, "I wish Mr. Meiser could be here today. He said cars were his passion. Can you imagine how thrilled he'd be?"

Trixie nodded her head. "What do you suppose is going to happen to him?"

"I don't know," Jim replied. "Kowalski's story has been broken wide open, after all he admitted to you the other night. So the original charge of assault will undoubtedly be dropped after a hearing. Since Mr.

Meiser did escape from prison, he'll have some straightening out to do with the law before he's through."

"But he risked his life to save us," Honey said. "That has to be worth something."

"I'm sure it will be," Brian assured her. "The fact that he called the police as soon as Kowalski called him and told them exactly what was happening, so that the squad cars could be waiting at Memorial Park, is bound to work in his favor, too."

"I feel terrible about all the doubts I had about Mr. Meiser while Andy Kowalski had us in the back of the van," Trixie said. "I'd almost convinced myself that Mr. Meiser had arranged the whole thing so that he could drop off a phony bundle and get away, leaving us to—" She broke off with a shudder, refusing to think about what she and Honey would have been left to.

"The gruff exterior concealed a marshmallow heart, after all," Brian concluded.

"I hope we get a chance to thank him someday," Honey said.

Jim looked at his watch. "Right now, I'll thank you to get inside and man your stations," he said. "It's two minutes to sale time."

Trixie, Honey, Dan, and Di hurried inside. They barely had time to take their assigned places before the customers started to pour in.

The Bob-Whites had decided to take the various duties involved with the sale in rotation. Trixie and Honey took the first turn at the table by the door, with one girl adding up the customers' purchases and the other taking money and making change.

The others circulated among the tables, answering questions and, occasionally, serving as models for clothing being purchased for a son or daughter "about your size."

An hour into the sale, Trixie looked up and stared in amazement as what looked like a moving pile of rummage came toward her.

The rummage dropped to the table and the happy but embarrassed face of Mrs. Manning emerged from behind it. "Hello, again," she said cheerfully.

"Did you decide to take your contributions back?" Trixie asked, half-seriously.

"Oh, my, no," Mrs. Manning said. "These are all new things. Well, all new used things. You know what I mean. There's so much wonderful merchandise here!"

"What all are you buying?" Trixie asked, looking at the pile that Honey was sorting.

"Rags?" Honey asked, holding up a huge plastic bag full of cloth strips.

"Yes. Isn't it wonderful?" Mrs. Manning asked. "That bag has all the makings for a braided rug. Someone must have started it and lost interest after tearing up all the strips. My grandmother used to make braided rugs, and I always wanted to give it a try. Now I'm already halfway finished, and I haven't even started yet!"

Secretly, Trixie wondered if the project would ever be any closer to completion, but she didn't want to spoil Mrs. Manning's happiness.

"And look at this," Mrs. Manning continued, holding up a calendar wrapped in a plastic bag. "This calendar is for the year nineteen fifty-two. That's when I was married! Imagine finding a nineteen fifty-two calendar, after all these years!"

"Imagine," Honey said pleasantly, the corner of her mouth twitching.

"And this!" Mrs. Manning exclaimed, holding up a book with yellowed edges. "It's an almanac for nineteen sixty. That's the year my daughter was born. Won't she be thrilled to be able to read all about what the world was like when she was born?"

"I'm sure she'll be delighted," Honey said politely.

"Those are the most useful things I found," Mrs. Manning said, looking over her purchases. "The other things are just frivolous. This piece of needlework is so pretty, I just couldn't resist it, although I don't know quite where I'll hang it. And here's an ashtray that's a souvenir of the World's Fair in New York. Now, that could be worth a lot of money as an antique someday, and it won't take up much room, so I thought I'd just buy it and hold on to it. And this—Oh, dear, there are lots of people in line behind me. You'll just have to visit me someday, and I'll tell you about the rest of these things."

"We'd love to, Mrs. Manning," Honey responded warmly for both of them.

"Would you like some help carrying those things to the car?" Trixie asked as she handed Mrs. Manning her change.

"Oh, no, thank you, dear. I can manage. Good-bye. I hope to see you soon." As Mrs. Manning spoke, she once again disappeared behind her pile of purchases.

Trixie shook her head as she watched the woman walk out the door. "If we have another sale, we'll know where to go asking for donations," she said.

Honey giggled. "We'll hear the stories behind the purchases all over again, too."

The next customer was Mrs. Maurer, the woman who had contributed her children's books. She made Trixie keep her promise to tell all about the author of the Lucy Radcliffe mysteries.

"The author's real name is Mr. Appleton," Trixie said. "He's sandy-haired and mild-mannered, easily embarrassed. Just to look at him, you'd never guess he could write such exciting mystery stories."

"But you said you'd suspected him of being a murderer!" Mrs. Maurer reminded Trixie.

"That was dumb," Trixie reflected.

"It wasn't dumb; it was a dummy," Honey corrected her.

Trixie laughed. "That's right. You see, Mr. Appleton has a dummy named Clarence. It's one of those manikins you see in department stores. He uses it to help him work out some of the action scenes in the Lucy Radcliffe books."

"How interesting!" the woman said.

"But he didn't tell us that at first. He said his hobby was wrestling, and that's what he used Clarence for. Well, Mr. Appleton didn't look a thing like a wrestler, so we got suspicious. Then, one night, we saw Mr. Appleton having what looked like an argument with someone, and that someone suddenly plunged over a cliff!"

"Oh, my!" The woman gasped.

"He said it was Clarence, but we wondered if that was the truth." Trixie shrugged, realizing that the ending of her story was anticlimactic. "It was."

Mrs. Maurer clucked as she paid for her purchases and put her change in her handbag. "Imagine, two young people like you meeting the author of the Lucy Radcliffe books! That must have been so exciting for you!"

"It was," Trixie said again.

The woman said good-bye and left, and Trixie turned to her honey-haired friend. "Imagine what that woman would say if she knew about the real excitement that went on at the Pirate's Inn—about the ghostly galleon that appeared only after dark, with the figurehead of a woman who seemed to have tears running down her face!"

"Imagine what she'd say if she knew that just two nights ago we had both been held hostage in the back of a van by a dangerous criminal!" Honey retorted. "Sometimes I think we lead more exciting lives than Lucy Radcliffe ever dreamed of!"

"Lucy Radcliffe can have my share of the excitement for a while," Trixie said. "Once this sale is over, I want to spend a long, leisurely summer not doing a thing."

"That attitude will last until the next time you see something that looks a teeny, tiny bit suspicious. Then you'll yell, 'Mystery!' and off we'll go again," Honey said.

Trixie laughed. "I confess," she said. "I don't really believe I've sworn off mysteries, even for the rest of the summer. But speaking of 'off we go,' I think our hour is about up. It's our turn to supervise the car display and take bids on the Model A." Trixie beckoned across the auditorium to Dan and Di, who were to take their places behind the table.

"We'll send two of the boys inside," Honey promised as the girls gave up their chairs to their friends.

Outside, a crowd had gathered in the parking lot,

but most of the antique cars were standing deserted. Instead, people were clustered at the far end of the lot.

"What's going on?" Trixie asked nobody in particular as they reached the crowd.

"I hope nothing's wrong," Honey said.

The girls worked their way through the throng and soon discovered what it was that had attracted everyone's attention.

"Mr. Burnside started up the Stanley Steamer! Mart and Dan and Di will get their rides after all!" Trixie exclaimed delightedly. "But that isn't Mr. Burnside driving it! Why, it looks like—"

"Mr. Meiser!" Honey shouted.

The inventor turned when he heard Honey's voice. He waved, stopped the car, and climbed down. Mr. Burnside took his place behind the wheel.

"Just the young ladies I came to see," Mr. Meiser said. "I got waylaid, though. I haven't seen a Stanley in years, and I couldn't resist taking her for a short spin."

"Are you— Did the police—" Trixie hesitated, unsure how to finish her question. The appearance of Sergeant Molinson at Henry Meiser's side answered her question.

"I'm not a free man," Mr. Meiser said. "Not yet, anyway. I've been back in the Sleepyside Hospital for the past two days. Now the doctor has said I'm well enough to travel, and the sergeant, here, is taking me back to face the music."

Trixie felt her eyes brimming with tears. This was the man who had saved her life, and now, partly because of that, he was on his way back to jail.

"Say, now, why so glum?" Mr. Meiser asked.

"I—I'm just sorry we got you into so much trouble," Trixie stammered.

"The way I look at it, you girls got me out of the trouble I'd been making for myself for a long, long time. Thanks to you, I had no trouble making the police listen to my story. They know, now, that Kowalski was trying to steal my invention that night at the shop. They know I hit him in self-defense. Those charges will surely be dropped."

"There's not much chance he'll have to do any more time for the escape, either," Molinson added. "It will take a while to get things straightened out, but Henry Meiser will be back on the street before you know it."

"Back to my senses, too," Meiser added. "That's even more important. The business of not trusting anyone was what really made trouble for me, at the trial and before. There will always be Andrew Kowalskis in the world, but they aren't the overwhelming majority that I thought they were. Your brother was right—getting involved with other people is what life is all about.

"So you see, I actually stopped by today to thank you all and to say I'll probably be seeing you soon," the inventor concluded.

"You mean you're coming back to Sleepyside?" Trixie asked.

"I don't have much choice," Henry Meiser said with a grin. "Eileen finally put her foot down. She told me she won't uproot her children for me again, and she resigned as my secretary."

"Oh, that's too bad," Trixie said, unable to understand why he seemed to be so happy about the decision.

"At least, she agreed to interview replacements for me. As soon as she finds one, she'll stop being my employee—and start being my wife!" Henry Meiser's grin was that of the cat who swallowed the canary.

Trixie felt tears brimming in her eyes once again, but this time with happiness. "May we come and visit you?" she asked.

"We'll be counting on it," Mr. Meiser said. "I've applied for a patent on my invention. Once it's granted, I'll sell the rights to the highest bidder, and then I'll just sit back while the money rolls in. There'll be plenty of time for socializing then."

"The miser!" Trixie cried. "Mr. Meiser, we never did find out what that invention is! Can't you at least give us a hint?"

"I can do a lot more than that," the inventor said. "Nobody can beat me to the punch at this late date. The miser is a special carburetor. Do you know what a carburetor is?"

"It's what makes a Model A break down," Trixie replied, wondering how a new version of that invention could be worth any money.

Henry Meiser laughed. "Every car has a carburetor. It's the part that supplies the fuel mixture to the engine. In a way, it's the part that determines how much fuel the car uses. And with my miser, a car will use about one-third as much fuel as the carburetors now use."

"Whew!" Trixie breathed. "With the cost of gas these days. . . ."

"Exactly. People will be clamoring to have the miser in their cars. And the best part of my invention is that it can be added to existing cars at a fraction of the cost of buying a new car. It'll pay for itself in a few hundred miles."

The inventor didn't speak for a moment, while he looked about him. "In a few years," he said softly, "any car without a miser carburetor will belong right here at a sale like this."

"You mean as antiques?" Trixie asked.

Henry Meiser turned and looked at her with a sparkle in his eyes. "Nope," the inventor said. "As rummage!"

With a wave of his hand, he turned and walked away to the waiting squad car.

As the two girls watched him leave, Honey asked thoughtfully, "If you were an inventor, Trix, what would you invent?"

"That's easy, Honey," Trixie answered with a mischievous grin. "More mysteries, of course!"